ERNEST CLINE

BRIDGE TO BAT CITY

 A mostly true tall tale . . .

Illustrations by **MISHKA WESTELL**

Ⓛ Ⓑ
LITTLE, BROWN AND COMPANY
New York Boston

Text and illustrations copyright © 2024 by Dark All Day Inc.
Illustrations by Mishka Westell

Cover art © 2024 by Dark All Day Inc. Cover art by Ramona Kaulitzki. Cover design by Karina Granda. Cover copyright © 2024 by Hachette Book Group, Inc.
Interior design by Carla Weise.

Little, Brown and Company
Hachette Book Group
1290 Avenue of the Americas, New York, NY 10104
Visit us at LBYR.com

First Edition: April 2024

Little, Brown and Company is a division of Hachette Book Group, Inc. The Little, Brown name and logo are trademarks of Hachette Book Group, Inc.

The publisher is not responsible for websites (or their content) that are not owned by the publisher.

Little, Brown and Company books may be purchased in bulk for business, educational, or promotional use. For information, please contact your local bookseller or the Hachette Book Group Special Markets Department at special.markets@hbgusa.com.

Library of Congress Cataloging-in-Publication Data
Names: Cline, Ernest, author. | Westell, Mishka, illustrator.
Title: Bridge to bat city / by Ernest Cline ; illustrated by Mishka Westell.
Description: First edition. | New York : Little, Brown and Company, 2024. | Audience: Ages 8 and up. | Summary: After her mother's death, thirteen-year-old Opal moves to her uncle's farm where she befriends a group of orphaned, music-loving bats, and summons the courage to protect them from a mining company as she attempts to find them a new home.
Identifiers: LCCN 2023039510 | ISBN 9780316460583 (hardcover) | ISBN 9780316460804 (ebook)
Subjects: CYAC: Bats—Fiction. | Music—Fiction. | Friendship—Fiction. | Austin (Tex.)—Fiction. | Texas—Fiction. | LCGFT: Novels.
Classification: LCC PZ7.1.C59536 Br 2024 | DDC [Fic]—dc23
LC record available at https://lccn.loc.gov/2023039510

ISBNs: 978-0-316-46058-3 (hardcover),
        978-0-316-46080-4 (ebook)

Printed in the United States of America

LSC-C

Printing 1, 2024

For all my fellow Austinites
(including the winged ones)

1

THE BIG OLD
BEAUTIFUL CAVE

Once upon a time down here in Texas, in a part of the Lone Star State known as the Hill Country, hidden at the edge of a rolling green forest, there was this big old beautiful cave.

And this big old beautiful cave happened to be home to a big old beautiful mess of bats. Over a million of them. These furry little flying critters had called the big old beautiful cave their home for a long, long time—since way back before the land around there was named Texas or Mexico. Since back before there were any people around to give the land any sort of name at all.

Now, according to our encyclopedia, the scientific

way to refer to a caveful of furry little flying critters would've been to call them "a colony of Mexican free-tailed bats." But I thought it was a little
heartless to refer to them as a "colony," when it
was plain to see that what they really were was a
family. One big old beautiful bat family, made up
of thousands and thousands of smaller bat families. All kinds of families, made up of all kinds of
bats, all living together in peace and harmony, in
their big old beautiful cave way out there in the Hill
Country...

When I first learned about the bats and how
they lived, I remember feeling a might envious,
because they could do several things I'd always
dreamed of being able to do. Like fly. And stay up
all night, every night, until the sun came up, and
then snore the daytime away.

Because they slept during the day, to them the
evening was like our morning. And every morning
at sunset, the bats would all fly out of their big old
beautiful cave to hunt for food. They would stay
out most of the night, flying for miles in all directions while gobbling up mountains of moths and

mosquitoes and flies and such. These bats were all natural-born bug hunters, and each one of them would eat its own weight in the pesky things every night, night after night.

To them, all those bugs tasted better than barbecue. I know most folks are probably revolted by the idea of eating insects. But most folks think hot dogs are delicious, including yours truly, so it's probably best we don't judge. Never yuck anyone else's yum, as my mama used to say.

When they weren't soaring through the night sky, the bats preferred to hang upside down by their feet. That's why they lived on the ceiling of their big old beautiful cave, in their own little upside-down bat city, nestled into the rock. Living upside down was normal for the bats. From their perspective, they probably figured all of us humans were the ones who were living upside down.

Now, contrary to what you may have heard, bats are not blind. They can see just fine. But they can hear even better. Every bat is born with a pair of superpowered ears that it can swivel in any direction, and bats use their ears in conjunction with their voices to create a kind of natural sonar array, which they use to help them avoid obstacles, zero in on prey, and escape predators.

There were always plenty of mean old hawks and dumb old owls flying around out there hunting the bats for food, whenever they were out hunting bugs for food. Luckily, bats are the fastest mammals in the world, so they were usually able to outrun the mean old hawks and owls and other birds of prey. Usually. But not always.

Hunting and being hunted. It was their way of life.

Each morning at sunrise, after the bats had finished gorging themselves at the big all-you-can-eat Hill Country bug buffet, they would fly back home to the big old beautiful cave to feed their pups and tuck all of them in for the day. That evening, when the sun went back down, the bats would wake up and repeat the exact same routine all over again. Day after day. Night after night. Season after season. Until the temperature began to drop.

Bats are warm-blooded mammals, just like you and me, and since there were over a million of them living in the big old beautiful cave, their collective body heat could usually keep the whole place nice and toasty warm. But once winter arrived, it would get too cold outside at night for the bats to hunt, unless they wanted to run the risk of freezing solid in midflight. And the colder it got, the fewer insects there were around for them to eat, and they would quickly start to run out of food. When that happened, the whole colony would pack up and fly south for the winter, migrating just like a lot of birds tend to do. They usually took their winter vacation down in South Texas, or sometimes all the way across the border in Old Mexico, where the weather was much warmer, and where they could still find plenty of bugs to eat all winter long.

Bats aren't lucky enough to have jackets and winter coats to put on when it gets chilly out. But they do have a coat of fur on their bodies that helps keep them warm, and they can also wrap their furry little wings around their furry little bodies, which is sort of like having a built-in electric blanket.

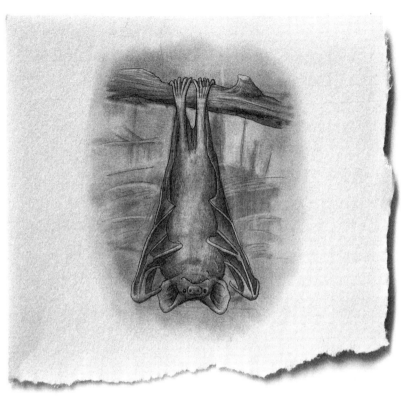

But the bats didn't have a permanent home down there, so they had to sleep in a different tree every night, or in some old, abandoned barn or other building, when they were lucky enough to find one. I figure they didn't mind roughing it down south for a few months every year, because they always knew it was only temporary. It was probably like going camping for them. And as soon as winter was over and the nights started to warm back up, the bats would all Boogie Back to Texas,* hightailing it north all the way back to their little home in the Hill Country.

* "Boogie Back to Texas" is the title of a great dance song by a band called Asleep at the Wheel. In my head, I would always picture the bats all singing that song in unison each spring as they flew north toward the Texas border, bound for home.

When they all finally made it back to the big old beautiful cave, they would pick up right where they'd left off and go right back to sleeping all day and bug hunting all night.

The bats followed this same routine, year after year, century after century, for countless generations. Until one summer, when a series of wild and weird events began to unfold that would change their lives—and mine—forever.

I know there may be a few folks out there who

doubt the veracity of this tale, but it did happen. My mama didn't raise no liars. Yes, I admit—I've told a tall tale or two. And I have been known to embellish a bit from time to time. But I was raised to believe that a good story is worthy of a little embellishment, and this here yarn I'm fixing to spin is my absolute favorite by a considerably wide margin. If I conflate a few dates or fudge a few facts, it ain't intentional. It's because all this stuff happened thirty or forty years ago, and old memories can fade just like old photographs. They can also get scratched up and worn out if you handle them too much. And if you don't keep them somewhere safe, you might lose them altogether. That's why I hope you'll hold on to this one for me.

Go ahead and pull up a chair, kick off your boots, and put up your feet. I'll tell all y'all exactly what occurred, to the best of my recollection.

The wildness and weirdness all began when a thirteen-year-old girl moved in right next door to the big old beautiful cave, and she and the bats became neighbors....

2

THE GIRL FROM LEVEL LAND

She was this weird little gal named Opal B Flats, and before she moved next door to the bats, she lived her whole life up in Lubbock, a windblasted outpost of humanity located up there in the middle of that endlessly flat and desolate rectangular region at the top of Texas known as "the Panhandle."

The Texas Panhandle is the rectangular part of the state at the top that looks like it could be the handle of a Texas-shaped frying pan.

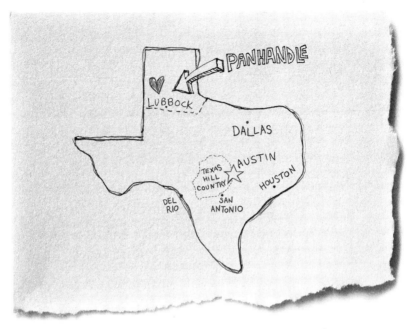

Opal figured it was probably just a cruel coincidence that her last name was Flats and she also happened to be born in the flattest place on God's green earth.

Folks would joke that it was so flat in Lubbock you could see for fifty miles in every direction—and if you stood on a tuna can, you could see for a hundred. Local legend had it that whenever a tree grew in Lubbock, someone would run right over and cut it down, so as not to spoil the breathtakingly boring view of absolutely nothing in every direction.

Her mama owned a big old Texas-shaped frying pan whose design had always confounded Opal, because its panhandle wasn't attached to the Panhandle! It was attached somewhere down around Del Rio. Such a missed opportunity. Anyway, Opal's mama would still use her Texas-shaped frying pan to make Texas-shaped corn bread. And Texas-shaped pancakes, using a Texas-shaped pancake mold small enough to fit inside the big Texas-shaped frying pan. Her mama would always use a blueberry to mark the spot where Lubbock was located, because that was home.

Opal never liked to refer to the part of Texas she lived in as "the Panhandle." She didn't think the name fit, because it failed to convey the mind-numbingly

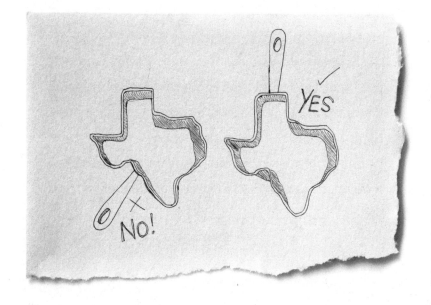

monotonous nature of the landscape around her. So one day she decided to come up with her own nickname for it: Level Land.

Sometimes she and her mama went to a farmers' market in a little town about thirty miles west of Lubbock with the name Levelland—as in "Level Land." Opal loved the name so much she decided to adopt it as her private nickname for the endlessly flat and even rectangular region she called home. Her mama adopted it, too, and neither one of them ever referred to it as "the Panhandle" again. Whenever Grandpa Filo and Uncle Roscoe drove up from the Hill Country to visit, she and her mama would greet them out in the driveway with shouts of "Welcome back to Level Land, y'all!"

If Opal had her druthers, the region formerly known as the Panhandle would've been officially relabeled Level Land on all the state maps. And the state highway patrol would've posted warning signs all around its borders that read:

TRAVELERS BEWARE!

y'all are fixin' to enter the desolation
known as level land,

≡ ≡

where everything and everyone is pretty much
on the level.

≡ ≡

(no gas or trees for the next however-many miles.
proceed at your own risk.)

Opal lived with her mama, Geraldine, who worked as a seamstress and a tailor. That's a fancy way of saying that she sewed things for a living. Most of her time was spent altering clothes to make them fit people better. But she occasionally created new pieces of clothing, too, that she designed and made herself, by stitching together elaborate mosaics of leftover fabric that she rescued from the trash bin at work. Every dress or shirt or suit she made was like a wearable work of art. Opal loved wearing outfits that her mother had made for her to school, even if some of the other kids always made cracks about them. She knew they were just jealous they couldn't get sweet custom threads like hers at Sears or Kmart.

Opal had never been a fan of store-bought clothes. She usually had a hard time finding anything in the girls' section that fit, because she was so big for her age. Her phys ed teacher had once described her as "kinda barrel-shaped." And "Flats is round" was a taunt she'd had hurled her way since kindergarten. But Opal never let those cracks bother her too much, because her mama was barrel-shaped, too, and Opal thought she was far and away the most beautiful woman in the world. She hoped she grew up to look just like her someday.

Opal's favorite outfit her mama had ever made her was the turquoise tuxedo she sewed Opal for her thirteenth birthday. It was created out of shiny pieces of fabric that made her look like she was wearing a stained-glass window or maybe a futuristic suit of armor. And her mama had stitched a silver capital O for *Opal* onto its lapel. Whenever Opal put it on, she never wanted to take it off. But she was also careful not to wear it too much, because she didn't want to wear it out.

The main thing you probably need to understand about Geraldine is that she wasn't just Opal's mama—she was also her favorite person in the whole wide world. And with good reason. Opal's mama wasn't just wicked funny, crazy beautiful, and sharp as a tack. She was also kind beyond measure, and she loved music just as much as Opal did. Which was saying something. Because Opal was a full-blown melomaniac.

In case you haven't heard that term before, it's a combination of the words *melody* and *maniac*. According to my dictionary, a melomaniac is "an individual who is inordinately and abnormally affected by musical or other tones." That described Opal to a T.

According to her mama, when Opal was a newborn, the only thing that would stop her incessant wailing and crying was the sound of music, so her mama just left the radio on all day long. And from the start, Opal's favorite musician was a fella named Buddy Holly, who happened to be from Lubbock, just like her. The local radio stations would play Buddy's songs all the time, on account of him being a local boy, and the sound of his voice always made little Opal's smile stretch from ear to ear.

When Opal got a little older, she learned that Buddy Holly used to live right there in her neighborhood, in a little red house over on Thirty-Ninth Street, just a few blocks away from the little blue house she shared with her mama. Opal would make a detour every morning on her way to school to walk by Buddy's old house, whistling the tune to one of his songs as she strolled past.

As she grew, Opal began to explore her mama's sizable record collection (which had a few of her daddy's old records mixed in there, too) and her musical horizons quickly broadened, and she started to listen to a lot of other kinds of music, too. But she never outgrew her first love. No matter how old she got, she would still find herself listening to Buddy Holly's music whenever she needed a little calming down or cheering up. "Rave On" or "That'll Be the Day" or "Not Fade Away" would always do the trick. And if it didn't, in a pinch she could always put on "Peggy Sue" and dance her cares away.

Ever since she was little, Opal had also loved to draw and doodle all the time, so when she was five, her mama bought her a hardbound sketchbook for her birthday. It was a big blue book filled with nothing but blank pages, and her mama told her she could put whatever she wanted to in there. At first Opal would just practice drawing her favorite cartoon and comic book characters in it. Then she started drawing little portraits of her favorite musicians in there, too, and she would write little mini biographies filled with interesting facts underneath her drawings of them, along with a list of her favorite songs and albums by each person or group. Then Opal started writing down the lyrics to her favorite songs on its pages, too, and before long she

* **Name:** Charles Hardin Holley aka Buddy Holly (1936–1959)
* **Born and raised in Lubbock, Texas (in the same neighborhood as me!)**
* **Attended J. T. Hutchinson Middle School (just like me!)**
* **Best Songs:** "Not Fade Away," "Rave On," "Oh Boy!," "Peggy Sue," "That'll Be the Day," "You're So Square (Baby, I Don't Care)"

was also using it as a kind of journal, notebook, and scrapbook, as well as a sketchbook. Opal called it her "scratchbook," and she carried it with her everywhere.

She was always drawing or writing in it, and when she saw an interesting article or photo in a newspaper or a magazine, she would cut it out and paste it in her scratchbook, too. When she filled all its pages, her mother bought her a new scratchbook. And then another. Opal would go through two or three of them a year. All her old scratchbooks were stored on a bookshelf in her bedroom. She had over a dozen of them now. Her current scratchbook was usually in her backpack, when it wasn't tucked under her arm or open in front of her.

When Opal was writing or drawing in her scratchbook, her mama referred to it as "scratchin'," and whenever she walked in and saw her daughter scratchin' away in her scratchbook it never failed to make her smile. Once in a while she would ask for Opal's permission to look through some of her old scratchbooks, and when Opal said yes (as she always did), her mama would sit down on the edge of her bed and spend hours looking through them, oohing and aahing and laughing and crying and sharing stories about the past inspired by all the hidden treasures found in their wrinkled pages.

Opal felt a special kinship with her mama, because she had a mile-wide weird streak running through her, too. They were like two weird little peas in a pod, and they always had been. They gave each other weird short haircuts, and they both wore weird vintage clothing they found in weird local thrift stores.

Most of the straitlaced folks in Lubbock didn't seem to know what to make of them. The general opinion among her peers at school had always seemed to be that Opal and her mama both looked weird, dressed weird, acted weird, talked weird, and were weird, and that just plain weirded people out. But that was just as fine as frog hair with Opal, and with her mama, too. They both agreed that being weird was way more fun and interesting than being average, normal, and as boring as bathwater.

Opal tried to follow her mama's example and embrace her weirdness, because she knew she really didn't have much choice. Being an oddball was in her blood, just as much as her love of music was. She issued from a long and distinguished line of weirdos and melomaniacs, on both sides of her family tree.

Opal's daddy was named Fred D Flats, but everyone called him Freddy, and if the stories I've heard about him are to be believed, Freddy Flats was a fairly weird fella, too. For starters, he had an uncanny ability to memorize song lyrics. He only needed to hear them once. Legend had it that by the time he graduated high school, he was able to recite the lyrics to hundreds of different songs. His friends used to play a game where they would spin the radio dial to try and find a song that would stump him, but somehow he always seemed to know the words to everything on every station.

Another weird thing about Fred D Flats was that his middle initial didn't stand for anything. His entire middle name was just the letter *D*, as in the musical note. As part of some silly long-standing family joke, everyone born into the Flats clan, including Opal, was given one of the first seven letters of the alphabet as their middle name, so it would sound like a musical note when folks said it aloud along with their surname. Her great-granddaddy was named Major F Flats III. Her granddaddy was Filo G Flats. Her daddy was Frederick D Flats. His little brother, her uncle, was Roscoe E Flats. And she was Opal B Flats.

Folks rarely found the musical-note-for-a-middle-name joke funny, even after Opal explained it. She thought it probably would've worked better with her mother's maiden name, which happened to be Sharp. But Opal liked being a Flats, and she didn't mind having a note for a middle name. It was a little reminder that she'd inherited her melomania from both sides of her family. The Sharps and the Flats.

Opal never even would've been born if it weren't for her parents' shared love of music. They met at a big music festival over in Dripping Springs. According to her mama, Waylon Jennings was up on the stage singing a song he wrote with Willie Nelson called "Good Hearted Woman" when her parents spotted each other in the crowd and locked eyes. It was love at first sight for both of them. Fred Flats and Geraldine Sharp got hitched about a month later, and Opal was born about a year after that.

Unfortunately, Opal's daddy died a few months before she was born, so she never even got to meet him. He got drafted and died in the Vietnam War.

When Opal asked her mama why they made him go over there to fight people he didn't even know, she said there was no point trying to make sense out of it, because nobody dying in any war had ever made a lick of sense. She said there were always other ways of resolving a dispute without resorting to killing folks.

Opal's mama had lost her own daddy in a war, too, in Korea. So Grandma Sharp had had to raise her daughter on her own, just like Opal's mama was now having to raise Opal on her own. Sometimes Opal wondered if that was just a cruel coincidence or the beginnings of some kind of family curse.

Grandma Sharp passed away when Opal was in kindergarten, so Opal could still remember her a little bit. Her first name was Eunice. Opal couldn't remember her other grandma at all. That was the one she was named after, her daddy's mama, Grandma Opal. She passed away before Opal was born, too, when her daddy was still in high school.

Opal's mama used to tell her that she'd inherited traits from both sides of her family. When Opal would ask which ones, her mama would always say the same thing.

"The Flats were weird and wistful and willful, and the Sharps were welcoming, wise, and a little weird, too," she would say. "And you, my sweet little girl, take after them both, in equal measure."

Opal was extremely proud of her ancestry and did her best to live up to it.

In first grade, Opal's eye doctor told her that she had an astigmatism and would need to start wearing corrective lenses to compensate for it. Then, he promised, she would be able to see writing on the chalkboard at school without having to squint all the time.

Opal hated the idea of wearing glasses at first, because she knew the other kids would start calling her "four-eyes." But then her mama told her she could get a pair of glasses just like the ones Buddy Holly wore. Suddenly, she was over the moon!

They had frames just like Buddy's for sale at the glasses store over at the mall, but the mean old saleslady behind the counter told her they were meant for boys to wear and that they would look awful on a girl. But they didn't! Opal looked at her reflection in the mirror, and she thought they made her look just like Buddy. And no one had ever looked cooler than him, except for maybe Elvis Presley or James Brown. Thankfully, her mama completely ignored the mean old saleslady and bought the Buddy Holly horn-rims for Opal anyway. She spent the whole ride home admiring them in the rearview mirror.

Of course, when she wore them to school the next day, it was open season. Everyone started calling her "Four-Eyed Flats." But Opal didn't care, because she knew how cool she looked in her horn-rims. And several of her teachers confirmed it when they told her she looked "just like Buddy Holly" in her groovy new spectacles. After that, when someone called her four-eyes, she just felt bad for them, because it meant the poor ignorant soul didn't know enough about music or style to recognize how ridiculously cool she looked. Which, in her humble opinion, was deeply uncool.

She got used to being ridiculed and ostracized at school, just like she'd gotten used to the dust storms and the depressing landscape. In Opal's experience, you could get used to just about anything, as long as you had plenty of good music to listen to, and someone you loved to listen to it with. Opal had both of those things, so she considered herself blessed.

For the most part, Opal's life up there in Level Land was calm and uneventful. But it did occasionally contain an element of danger. Because the endlessly flat landscape around Opal's hometown didn't just make the place look ugly. It also made it windy. And I mean crazy windy. Out of nowhere, these horrendous windstorms would suddenly roll in over the horizon and descend over the whole town, forcing everyone to seek shelter indoors. Sometimes the wind would be strong enough to blow Opal right off her feet, and she'd have to grab on to the nearest light pole or handrail and hold on for dear life until the storm subsided, to avoid getting blown away like a tumbleweed.

Then one day, just a few weeks after she turned thirteen, a different kind of storm rolled into Opal's life that blew so strong she lost her grip. And she did get blown away like a tumbleweed, all the way out of her home and her life and everything she'd ever known up there in Level Land.

3

GOING UP TO THE SPIRIT IN THE SKY

Opal knew something was wrong when she got home from school that afternoon and she didn't see her mama's car in the driveway. Uncle Roscoe's old red Rambler station wagon was parked there instead. He lived halfway across the state, way down in the Hill Country, and was usually able to visit them only a few times a year, usually around the holidays. But it wasn't a holiday. It was just a random Monday in late May. Opal still had nine more days of school left before she finished the seventh grade and started summer vacation.

As Opal continued walking toward the house, she spotted her uncle sitting on the steps leading up to the front porch. He was hunched over with his face in his hands, so he didn't spot Opal right away. But she knew who it was before she even saw his face, because he was wearing the same faded denim overalls he always wore. And he also had on his battered old white cowboy hat, which had a little square computer circuit board attached to its band in the front. Her uncle had added that personal touch after he inherited the hat from his daddy.

Uncle Roscoe finally looked up when he heard her approaching footsteps, and that was when she saw that he'd been crying. He'd taken off his glasses to wipe away his tears, and he quickly put them back on. They were round with wire frames, like the ones John Lennon used to wear, and their thick lenses magnified his pupils, making them appear much larger than they actually were.

"Hey, Opal," he said, once he found his voice. He took off his hat and tried to give her a smile, but his mouth refused to cooperate and he just ended up tightly pursing his lips. Opal didn't even have to ask him what was wrong. She could already tell by the look on his face that something bad must've happened to her mama.

She slid her backpack off and gently set it down on the ground. Then she took a seat on the steps beside him and waited.

Her uncle sat there in silence for a moment, struggling to find words. Then he took something out of his jacket pocket and held it out to her. It was an Atari cartridge with a bright red label that had the word *MEGAMANIA* printed on it. Opal took it with both hands and whispered thank you.

Uncle Roscoe was the one who had given Opal her Atari 2600 game console, as a gift for her ninth birthday. And ever since then, whenever he came up to visit them for any reason, he would always bring along a new Atari game for Opal, and then the two of them would usually stay up way too late playing it together. This was the first time she wasn't excited about receiving a new game from him, because she was so worried about why he was there.

She put the game into her own jacket pocket and waited.

Uncle Roscoe cleared his throat. Then, as gently

as he could, he explained that her mama had suffered a stroke caused by a blood clot in her brain. She'd collapsed earlier that morning at the tailor shop where she worked, and they'd rushed her to the hospital in an ambulance. The hospital called Uncle Roscoe because he was the person listed as her emergency contact, and he'd just spent the last five hours driving up to Lubbock as fast as he could, so he could be there waiting for Opal when she got home from school and they could go to the hospital together. He told Opal he didn't want her to hear the bad news about her mama from anyone else, and he also didn't want Opal to be alone or with strangers when she went in to see her.

Opal was extremely grateful to her uncle for all of this, but she was in such a state of shock she wasn't sure if she ever managed to say so out loud. She only remembered clutching his hand in silence during the long drive to the hospital. She also remembered hearing him promise to stick around and take care of her until her mama got better.

But her mama wasn't going to get any better. The doctors said there wasn't anything they could do to help her and that she probably didn't have much longer to live. Opal refused to believe them. She sat up with her mama all that night, but she never regained consciousness, and she passed away quietly the following morning while Opal was holding her hand.

When she realized that her mama had stopped breathing, Opal felt the most painful feeling she'd ever felt. A piercing hollowness that cored out her heart and her chest and her limbs and left her feeling empty all the way through.

I know this part of the story is terribly sad, and that now you're probably feeling awful for Opal, because I am, too, just thinking back on it. That was one of the worst moments of her entire life. And the next few days weren't going to be any picnic, either. But once Opal made it through them, her luck would change for the better, and her weird and wondrous destiny would begin to reveal itself. Just wait and see....

In the days and nights that followed, Opal realized that Uncle Roscoe had done her one of the biggest kindnesses of her life by giving her that copy of *MegaMania* the night before her mama passed. Because she spent nearly every waking moment of the next few mostly sleepless days playing it, while listening to Buddy Holly's *Greatest Hits* over and over again on her boom box. This kept her brain and her hands completely occupied, and that was enough to keep her from slipping down any further into the depths of despair.

But unfortunately she couldn't play *MegaMania* nonstop. Her uncle kept dragging her out of the house, to go cry her eyes out for a few hours in some church or cemetery while they attended her mama's memorial, funeral, and subsequent burial. Those were a couple of the hardest days Opal ever had to live through.

Her mama's funeral wasn't a big affair. Her friends from work all came to pay their respects, and a bunch of her regular customers did, too. They were all wearing colorful patchwork clothing that she'd made for them. And so were Opal and Uncle

Gemstone Jean Jacket

Turquoise Tuxedo

Roscoe. She was dressed in her turquoise tuxedo, and he was wearing his gemstone jean jacket her mama had given him the previous Christmas, even though he said it made him feel ridiculous.

When the pastor opened up the floor, a bunch of people went up to the lectern one after the other to say a few words about her mama, about how much joy and kindness and beauty she and her clothing had brought into their lives, and how badly they were going to miss her. It was heartbreaking for Opal to hear these things, because each one of them seemed to make her miss her mama even more, but she was still grateful to have heard them.

Her uncle walked up there and tried to say a few words, too, but he was too choked up to get any out. He was able to manage only a few strangled sobs, while he stood there with his gemstone jean jacket glittering under the lights. Finally he just laid his right hand on her mama's casket for a moment and then sat back down next to Opal without saying anything. Opal still gave him a big hug anyway for trying.

Opal knew she probably wouldn't be able to get any words out, either, if she went up there and tried to talk about her mother. Thankfully she'd planned ahead. She'd brought along the boom box her mama had given her for her thirteenth birthday a few weeks earlier. She carried it up and set it on the lectern, then pressed play on the tape she'd made earlier that morning. It had only one song on it, recorded over and over again on both sides of the cassette. It was the song her mama had always told her she wanted to be played at her funeral someday: "Spirit in the Sky" by Norman Greenbaum.

Her mama always used to sing along with the lyrics whenever it came on the radio, and Opal would always chime in and echo her, singing the backup vocals in a high-pitched falsetto.

Her mama especially loved the part that went: "When I die and they lay me to rest, gonna go to the place that's the best."

That line always made her mama happy for some reason, and she would belt it out at the top of her lungs.

When the song was over, Opal just let the tape roll, and in a few seconds the song started over again from the beginning. Opal let it continue to play over and over again on a continuous loop for the rest of the ceremony.

They buried Opal's mama right alongside her daddy and all four of her grandparents in the Lubbock cemetery. Buddy Holly was buried there, too, just a stone's throw away, so Opal knew her mama was being laid to rest in good company. That didn't make her miss her mama any less, though.

Opal and Uncle Roscoe were the last two people to leave her mama's grave. After everyone else was gone, they both just stood there staring down at their family members' side-by-side tombstones. Both of Opal's parents, and all four of their parents, too. All the Flats and Sharps were lined up in a row there in front of them, like keys on a piano.

Her mama's daddy had been buried here first. After her mama had Opal's daddy buried next to him, Grandpa Filo had arranged for he and his wife's ashes to be interred here, too, so that they could be laid to rest alongside their son. Now her mama was buried alongside him, too.

Opal tried not to look at the empty patch of ground beside her parents' graves that she knew was reserved for her. There was an empty spot over by Uncle Roscoe's parents that she figured was probably set aside for his grave, too. She tried not to look at it, either. She was already sad enough.

When everyone else had been gone for a while and Opal and her uncle both finally managed to stop crying for a little bit, he crouched down to look her in the eye and asked her if she wanted to come and live with him on the Flats family farm down in the Hill Country.

Opal didn't need to think it over. She nodded yes right away, because she loved Uncle Roscoe and she knew he loved her back, and that he'd do his best to take care of her.

She also knew he was just asking her out of kindness, because he was the only family she had left, and they both knew she had nowhere else to go.

So off she went, tumbling away like a tumbleweed on the winds of fate. They scooped her up and carried her off, all the way out of Level Land and into the unknown.

4

RAMBLIN' WITH UNCLE ROSCOE

Uncle Roscoe drove a rusted red 1963 AMC Rambler Classic station wagon that he called the "Red Rambler." Whenever he drove somewhere in it, he never referred to it as *driving*. He called it *rambling*.

"Do you need me to ramble you somewhere?" he'd ask. And if you said yes, he'd say, "Okay, then let's get ramblin'!" Or "Are you ready to ramble?"

Uncle Roscoe's Red Rambler had a stereo with a cassette deck in it, and a huge case full of music tapes sitting on the front seat, and he told Opal she could be the DJ for their entire road trip. She got to spend the whole ride picking out one song after another. She and Uncle Roscoe would sing along when they knew the words and hum along when they didn't, and the time began to fly by along with the miles.

Opal listened to her Buddy Holly's *Greatest Hits* tape in its entirety at least three or four times. In a row. But her uncle didn't even complain once, because he loved Buddy's music almost as much as Opal did.

Uncle Roscoe was only ten years older than Opal, so he was just twenty-three when he took her in and became her legal guardian. It had to be a little scary for him, because he was still just a kid himself, and he didn't have the first clue how to be a parent. He probably wasn't sure if he was cut out for it.

To be truthful, Opal wasn't sure if Uncle Roscoe was cut out to be a farmer, either. His heart just didn't seem to be in it. His real passion was messing with computers. They were all he ever talked about, and he spent all his free time learning how to use them. After he finished high school, he'd been planning to go off and study computer programming at the University of Texas, but then his daddy—Filo,

Opal's grandpa—got sick, and so after he graduated, Uncle Roscoe had to stay home to take care of him and help run the farm. The following year, Grandpa Filo passed away, and he left the Flats family farm to Uncle Roscoe.

Opal had seen Grandpa Filo only a handful of times when she was little. She remembered him as a sweet old man who pulled marbles out of her ears and then gave them to her as presents. Grandpa Filo and Uncle Roscoe used to ramble up to Lubbock together every year to spend Thanksgiving with Opal and her mama, until Grandpa got too frail to make the trip. After that, Uncle Roscoe would ramble up to Lubbock alone to visit them. Grandpa Filo would still call them on the phone occasionally, and he would always invite them to come down to the Flats farm for a visit sometime, but they never did.

Opal knew her mama loved Grandpa Filo and Uncle Roscoe dearly, but she also knew it was kinda hard for her to be around them, because they both reminded her so much of Opal's daddy. To her, they both looked and sounded just like an older and a younger version of her late husband. And visiting them both at the farm where he'd grown up might've been too much for her tender heart to bear. Opal figured that was why they'd never made the trip. But she'd grown up hearing stories about the Flats family farm down in the Hill Country, and now all of a sudden she was moving there. Thinking about it made her feel a little homesick, so she tried not to think about it at all.

The five-hour drive down to the farm was the longest road trip Opal had ever been on. During the journey, she kept glancing over her shoulder at all her boxed-up belongings piled in the back. Everything she owned in the world was back there. All her clothes and shoes and books and records and games. All the remnants of her old life back in Level Land.

A few hours into their journey, they stopped at a Whataburger for lunch, and while they were eating at a picnic table out front, Opal asked Uncle Roscoe if he liked being a farmer. The question seemed to catch him off guard. He took off his hat and scratched

his scalp with his fingernails a few times before putting it back on. Then he pushed his glasses up his nose with his index finger. He performed this ritual sometimes when he was nervous or uncomfortable.

"No, Opal," he replied, letting out a long sigh. "I have to confess that I *do not* like being a farmer. Not one bit. I disliked doing farmwork when I was a kid, and I still dislike it now." He glanced upward at the clear blue sky overhead. "But I loved my folks, and I missed them to pieces, and deep down I knew they wouldn't have wanted me to just up and sell the place the second they were both gone. That farm has been in our family for generations, so…" He shrugged. "So I didn't really feel like I had much choice. There was no one else to tend the crops or feed the livestock. So instead of going off to college at UT, I stayed put on the farm and did my best to keep it going."

He said he'd been doing that for the past three years now, and it sounded to Opal like it was really starting to wear on him. It made her feel a little guilty, because now, on top of taking care of the farm and all the animals on it, he'd just volunteered to take care of her, too.

"I'm really grateful to you for taking me in, Uncle Roscoe," she told him. "I know you didn't have to."

"Oh, hush now with all that nonsense," he replied, shaking his head. Then he reached across the picnic table to give her tiny hand a squeeze.

"We're family, you and me," he told her. "And that means we stick together. Always. Through thick and thin, frown or grin, until we win. Okay, ace?"

Opal smiled a little and nodded. Uncle Roscoe smiled and nodded back. Then he changed the subject by asking her if she wanted a milkshake, like that was the end of it.

Once they finished eating and got back on the road, Uncle Roscoe turned on the Red Rambler's radio, and a really good song came on that Opal had never heard before. It was called "If You Want to Sing Out, Sing Out" by Cat Stevens. It's one of those songs that makes you feel happy and sad at the same time, so it was the perfect song for Opal to hear in that moment, because it captured just how she was feeling.

Happy and sad at the same time.

As they continued to ramble south, the flat and desolate landscape Opal had known all her life began to disappear, slowly giving way to more mountainous terrain as they reached the outskirts of the Texas Hill Country, which is roughly where the Southwest meets the Southeast.

At one point they rambled past an old abandoned schoolhouse alongside the highway, and the sight of it made Opal gasp and turn to her uncle in a panic.

"Oh no!" she cried. "I forgot all about school! Don't I need to go back and finish seventh grade?"

Uncle Roscoe smiled at her reassuringly and shook his head.

"No, honey, you don't," he replied. "I spoke with your principal before we left, and he agreed to release you for summer vacation a few days early. So you don't need to worry about going back to school until the fall. Okay?"

Opal nodded and let out a sigh of relief. "Thanks, Uncle Roscoe."

"You got it, pal."

He rambled on down the highway in silence for a few minutes before something else occurred to him.

"Listen, I'm sorry you didn't get a chance to say goodbye to any of your friends at school. I should've asked you if you wanted to do that before we left."

"Oh, don't sweat it, Uncle Roscoe," she replied. "I didn't have any."

"Any what?"

"Friends," she replied. "To say goodbye to." She shrugged. "I never fit in at school. It's been that way since kindergarten. The other kids don't like the way I look or dress. They all think I'm a weirdo."

He glanced over at her. He suddenly had a very serious look on his face.

"That's the thing they never tell you when you're a kid," he said, shaking his head. "The hardest subject in school is the one they never grade you on—trying to fit in with all the other kids and get them to like you. That's a heck of a lot harder than algebra. I never quite got the hang of it, either. My classmates thought I was a weirdo, too. And you know what? They were right! And for that fact I shall be eternally grateful."

He pointed a finger at her.

"You should wear your weirdness like a badge of honor, Opal," he proclaimed. "Nothing is more boring than being normal. Trust me. You'll see. It's always the weird folks who tell the best stories, make the best music, create the best art, and cook the best food! Weirdos make the world go round!"

He honked the Rambler's horn a few times to make his point. This drew glares from several of the other drivers around him, and he gave each of them a smile and a friendly wave. Then he turned back to Opal.

"And there's nothing wrong with the way you look, either," he said. "You're cute as a button and always have been!" Then he lowered his voice and exaggerated his Texas accent before adding, "And I'll fight any man or woman who says otherwise!"

Opal usually loved it when he changed his voice like that, because it made him sound just like Grandpa Filo. She knew he was trying to cheer her up, but she wasn't in the mood to feel anything but rotten at the moment. And probably for the foreseeable future.

"Thanks, Uncle Roscoe," she said. "But you're my uncle. You're biased."

"I'm *right*, is what I am!" he replied in the same crotchety-old-man voice, slamming his fist down on the dashboard in mock anger. "Don't you contradict me now, girl! I won't have that!"

It was touch-and-go there for a second. He almost made Opal laugh. Not quite, but almost. He did make her grin a little, though. Just a little. But that was enough for Uncle Roscoe. He took it as a good sign.

He turned on the radio, and there was another good sign, because it was Willie Nelson singing "On the Road Again," and they both began to sing along with him as the Red Rambler continued to ramble on down the highway.

5

FLATS IN THE HILL COUNTRY

When they finally arrived at the farm that evening, it was right around sunset, and the bands of clouds that stretched across the sky were turning a hundred different shades of red, orange, and violet. It was unlike any sunset Opal had ever seen up in Level Land. It took her breath away.

Up ahead, on the left, Opal spotted a rusted old mailbox with the name *FLATS* painted on the side.

"Welcome to your new home, Opal!" Uncle Roscoe said. "We made it." He motioned proudly to the fields of corn and beans surrounding them. "This farm has been in our family since 1865, when they first emigrated here from Germany."

"Wow," Opal replied, gazing around in wonder. "That's a really long time."

Uncle Roscoe pulled his Rambler alongside the mailbox and retrieved a big stack of letters from inside. Then, without even glancing at them, he stuffed them into the glove box as quickly as he could. But not before Opal noticed that several of the envelopes were red and had the words *PAST DUE BILL—FINAL WARNING* printed on them. Opal pretended not to notice.

Uncle Roscoe turned off the paved road and onto a long gravel driveway that led up to an old white farmhouse in the distance, with a faded red barn just beyond it. As they approached the house, they passed half a dozen hand-painted wooden signs posted alongside the driveway. All of them said the same thing: THIS FARM IS NOT FOR SALE!

ESPECIALLY NOT TO MUCKERNO LIMESTONE! a few of them added at the bottom.

"What's with all the signs, Uncle Roscoe?" Opal asked.

"Muckerno Limestone has been trying to buy this land for ages," he replied. "So they can blast a

ESPECIALLY NOT TO MUCKERNO LIMESTONE!

THIS FARM IS NOT FOR SALE!

bunch of giant holes in the ground to dig up limestone, and poison the rivers, and kill off all the wildlife." He smiled reassuringly at her. "That is never, ever gonna happen. Selling this farm to them is just about the last thing I'd ever do. But they refused to take no for an answer, so I posted those signs to make my position clear. So far, they seem to be working, because those guys haven't been back to bother me since I put them up a few week ago."

Opal was about to respond when, out of the corner of her eye, she spotted an enormous flock of blackbirds flying directly overhead. The sky was suddenly filled with these tiny winged creatures, all of them silhouetted against the violet rays of the setting sun. But they weren't moving like any flock of birds she'd ever seen.

She leaned her head out of the Rambler's open passenger window to get a better look at them, and that was when she noticed the strange jagged outline of their wings and the odd noise they were making. It sounded as if they were squeaking instead of chirping....

Opal let out a frightened shriek and yanked her head back inside the car. Then she rolled up the window as quickly as she could, before sliding across the seat to clutch her uncle's right arm.

"Uncle Roscoe?" she whispered. "Are those *bats*?"

He stopped the Rambler and gave her a sheepish look, as if he'd been dreading this moment for some time.

"Yes, Opal," he replied. "They're bats. But don't worry; those furry little flying critters are as friendly as can be, and they're also completely harmless. We never told you about them because we were afraid you wouldn't want to visit...."

Opal didn't hear a word he said after *bats*. She was terrified of bats. Of course, the only time she'd ever seen a bat before was in some scary movie, or in a spooky cartoon like *Scooby-Doo*. This was the first time she'd ever seen a bat in real life. And now she was suddenly seeing about a million of them, all at once, up close and personal.

"Are any of them vampire bats?" she asked, gazing up at them in horror. "Do they bite you on the neck and suck out your blood?"

"No, of course not," he replied, chuckling. "They're furry little Mexican free-tailed bats." He leaned out his own window to smile up at them. "They're our friends, and our neighbors, too! They live in a big old beautiful cave just over that hill yonder, at the edge of the forest. If you like, we can walk over there tomorrow around sundown and watch them fly out for the night. They all leave the cave at the same time, streaming up into the sky one after the other, like a big old bat parade across the heavens. It's quite a sight to see, I promise you."

Opal thought it over for about half a second, then shook her head.

"No thank you!" she replied curtly. "I think I'll pass, Uncle Roscoe."

Vampire bats are found in Mexico, Central America, and South America, while free-tailed bats are found all over the world. One drinks blood; the other eats bugs. Big difference, y'all!

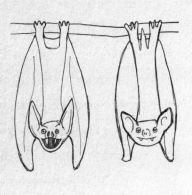

"Suit yourself, scaredy-cat," Uncle Roscoe said, ruffling her hair. "But you shouldn't believe everything you see in the movies. Bats are just about the best neighbors a farmer could wish for. We're lucky to have them around."

Opal eyed her uncle suspiciously, but he didn't appear to be joking.

"*Lucky?*" she repeated, leaning forward to peer up through the windshield at the endless stream of bats that continued to zoom overhead. "How is *this* lucky? It's like a plague of locusts."

He scrunched up his face at her. "No, it ain't!" he said. "It's the exact opposite. We would never have a plague of locusts around here, because all of those bats up there would eat them in about five minutes flat. That's what they do! Every night at sunset, a million of those bats fly out over all of these fields and spend the whole night gobbling up tons and tons of skeeters and flies and moths and all manner of agricultural pests! Every night, night after night, Opal!"

He smiled up at the torrent of bats through the Rambler's windshield.

"Thanks to our hungry little bat neighbors up there, the farmers around here never have to spray their crops with nasty pesticides to keep bugs from eating them all up. Because the bats eat *them* all up! And as a result, our beans and corn and squash

and tomatoes and cucumbers and strawberries all grow big and beautiful and delicious, year after year." Then, chuckling, he added: "Unless, of course, your uncle screws up the tilling, or the planting, or the fertilizing, or the weeding. All of which have been known to happen from time to time."

He told Opal that he tried to show the bats his gratitude whenever the opportunity arose. He always gave them a friendly wave whenever he saw them flying overhead. And if a few of the bats got caught out in a thunderstorm and it started raining too hard for them to fly home, he would throw open the doors to his barn so the bats could roost in there until the storm was over.

When the bats flew south each winter, Uncle Roscoe missed them something terrible. He told Opal that the farm just felt like a lonelier place without his furry little friends flying around. And each spring when the bats returned from their winter vacation, he would rush out to greet them and welcome them home, grateful to have them back to protect his crops for another year.

After Opal heard all of that, the bats suddenly didn't seem quite so scary to her anymore. Now she was kind of excited about having a million furry little flying critters as her new neighbors.

When they finally pulled up to the house and Opal climbed out of the Rambler, she felt like she was stepping into an old photograph. Specifically, an old photograph of her daddy standing in front of the very same house when he was a little boy. It was one of the pictures of him that used to hang in her mama's living room. Now Opal realized she was standing right where her father had stood when that photo was taken. Somehow this made the Flats family farm feel like a friendly and familiar place to Opal, even though it was her first time being there.

The house looked about a hundred years old on the outside, so the inside was kind of a shock. It looked more like a computer store than a farmhouse. Uncle Roscoe had computers, computer parts and peripherals, and books and magazines about computers piled on just about every flat surface, including the floor.

"Sorry for the mess," he said as he began moving boxes to clear a path through the living room. "I didn't have time to clean up before I left. Say, are you hungry? I can make some spaghetti if you like."

"No thanks, Uncle Roscoe," Opal said. "I'm still full of Whataburgers. And I'm pretty worn out from—"

Before Opal could finish her next sentence, she was overcome by an enormous yawn.

"I second that emotion," Uncle Roscoe said. "I'm

pretty worn out, too. Come on. Follow me upstairs, and I'll show you to your new digs."

He picked up her suitcases and led her up the creaky old staircase and then down the creaky old hallway to her new bedroom. The floor in there was awful creaky, too. Uncle Roscoe explained that it used to be her daddy's room when he was a boy, and that made Opal feel at home there right away, even though his things were long gone. Now the room was nearly empty, save for a creaky old spring bed, a nightstand with an old clock radio on it, and an antique wardrobe over in the corner. The faded and peeling wallpaper was a repeating pattern of atomic-age astronauts, space stations, and rocket ships.

There were also a bunch of empty cardboard computer boxes piled everywhere, but Uncle Roscoe quickly tossed them out into the hallway. Then he kissed Opal good night and told her he'd be in his room right down the hall if she needed anything. She gave him a thumbs-up. He returned it and then departed, closing the door behind him.

Opal quietly unpacked her things and put them in the wardrobe. Then she tiptoed across the floor and lay down on the creaky old spring bed. She stared up at the ceiling for a while, thinking about her daddy lying in the same bed when he was her age, staring up at the same ceiling.

Opal suddenly missed her mama very badly. And to her surprise, she found herself missing her home back in Lubbock, too. But she didn't let herself cry, because she didn't want Uncle Roscoe to hear it and think she was sad about having to come here and live with him. Because she wasn't. At all.

Opal continued to stare up at the ceiling for a little while, thinking about her mama and her daddy, and how the two of them were finally together again now that they were both up in heaven. She pictured them sitting together on a cloud, catching up on lost time, which made her feel a whole lot less sad. So she kept right on picturing it, until she finally drifted off to sleep.

6

OUT OF THIS WORLD

During the night, Opal had one of the strangest experiences of her life.

She was awoken from a deep sleep by a strange whistling sound that seemed to be coming from somewhere up above her, beyond the cracked plaster ceiling over her bed. It sounded like someone was up in the attic, playing one long, shrill note on a flute. And there was a ringing in her ears that just wouldn't go away.

Opal sat straight up in bed and looked around the room in bewilderment. A bright beam of moonlight was pouring in through the open window—at least, she thought it was moonlight at first. She glanced over at the ancient clock radio on the night-stand, and its glowing radium dial showed it was 3:33 AM.

Opal knew she should be frightened, but she felt strangely calm. She quietly slid out of bed and tip-toed over to the window.

When she peered outside, she realized that the moon wasn't even out. It had already set. All the bright light pouring into the room wasn't moonlight after all. It was coming from something else—something

big and shiny that was hovering up in the sky, directly over the empty field of grass adjacent to the farmhouse.

It was a giant metal disk, as big as a whole football field. To Opal, it looked like two giant stainless-steel mixing bowls welded together at the lip, with a ring of bright blue lights running all the way around the outside.

Opal immediately recognized it as a flying saucer, because she'd seen plenty of them before, in the old black-and-white science-fiction movies she used to watch with her mama on late-night television.

Opal *also* knew that flying saucers weren't just make-believe things from the movies, because her mama had seen a bunch of real ones when she was a little girl. Now Opal was seeing one, too, and as she stood there at the window staring at it, all she could think about was her mama's story.

One night, after they'd just finished watching *The Day the Earth Stood Still* together, Opal asked her mama if flying saucers were real. To her surprise, her mama replied, "Yes, baby girl. They absolutely are. And I know so for a fact, because when I was little like you, me and your grandma saw a whole mess of flying saucers zooming right over this very neighborhood. And we weren't the only ones, either. Half the folks in town saw them, every night for over a week."

It's true. You can look it up. Way back in August of 1951, there was practically a flying-saucer parade over Lubbock. They called them the Lubbock Lights. A bunch of folks saw them, including three science professors over at Texas Tech. And a boy named Carl snapped a bunch of photos of the glowing saucers that were reprinted in *Life* magazine the following year.

FUN FACT: Six years later, in November of 1957, there were a whole mess of UFO sightings over in Levelland, too. How weird is that?

Opal's mama told her that it wasn't just a bunch of circular lights that she saw up in the sky that night. She distinctly saw fourteen flying saucers moving across the night sky in formation. She said she'd never seen anything like them, before or since.

There was one other detail her mama shared with her about that night back in 1951. A supremely weird detail that had never made it into any of the news stories published about the Lubbock Lights.

She told Opal that a few seconds after they passed over her house, the formation of flying saucers suddenly stopped and hovered directly over a house a few blocks away. It was the house where fourteen-year-old Buddy Holly lived with his parents. The lead flying saucer shined a bright beam of blue light directly down on Buddy's house for a few seconds, before the entire formation zoomed off again, disappearing over the horizon in a blink, without ever making any sound at all.

"I don't know what those flying saucers were," she told her daughter. "Or where they came from. But I know they're real. And I know they must be up to something...."

Opal remembered watching her mama turn as white as a sheet when she recounted the story. Opal could tell from her tone of voice that she wasn't joking about any of it. Ever since then, she'd known that there really were flying saucers out there somewhere flying around. But she'd never expected to see one herself.

And now that she *was* seeing one, she still couldn't quite believe it....

As she continued to stare out the window at the silvery disk hovering there over the field, she noticed that the high-pitched whistling sound she'd heard earlier had gradually faded away. Now the night had gone completely silent. Even the crickets and the frogs had all clammed up.

Then something else happened that Opal couldn't explain. One second, she was standing there at her bedroom window, staring out at the flying saucer. Then, in the blink of an eye, she was suddenly standing out there in the field, directly underneath it!

She was looking straight up at its underside, into a blue beam of light that was shining directly down onto her. Opal was disoriented, but she still didn't feel afraid. She tried to raise her right hand to shield her eyes from the light, only to discover that she couldn't move her arm or her hand or any other part of her body. She was frozen in place like a statue.

A second later, the beam of bright blue light abruptly shut off and she was suddenly able to move again. Once her eyes adjusted, Opal glanced upward, just in time to see the flying saucer slowly tip over onto its side. Then it shot straight upward, like a bullet fired from a gun, and disappeared into the starry night sky in a blink, without making a sound. That was the last she ever saw of it.

Opal stood there in stunned silence for a moment, listening to the rapid beating of her heart. Then the darkness around her suddenly exploded with sound, as all the crickets and frogs started to make noise again all at once, and the sudden cacophony scared the living daylights out of her.

She ran back into the house, through the wide-open front door. Then she slammed it shut behind her, locked it, and sprinted up the stairs. She could hear Uncle Roscoe snoring softly in his room. He'd never even woken up. She considered waking him up now, to tell him what had just happened. But she wasn't sure if he'd believe her. She could hardly believe it herself. Besides, she suddenly felt so sleepy she could barely stand up.

She returned to her room and crawled back into bed. Then she glanced over at the old clock radio on the nightstand again. Now it said the time was 5:41 AM, which didn't make any sense to her. Somehow, over two whole hours had passed since that whistling sound had woken her up. But to her it felt like she'd been awake for only a few minutes.

Opal decided she was too tired to think straight, so she closed her eyes, and a few seconds later she was fast asleep.

When she woke up the next morning, Opal wasn't sure what to make of her scattered memories of the previous night. Maybe the whole thing had been a dream? An extremely vivid one.

She threw back the covers and swung her feet out of bed. They were both covered in dirt and grass stains, apparently as a result of prancing around barefoot out in that field under a flying saucer the night before.

I must've been sleepwalking, she told herself. Even though she had no history of it. And all the stuff she remembered about a flying saucer shining a beam of light down onto her had to be the remnants of some crazy nightmare she must've been having *while* she was sleepwalking.

Sure. That had to be it. A sleepwalking nightmare that somehow felt completely real. Probably triggered by her intense grief over the loss of her mother, combined with her anxiety about moving to a new place. But she was awake now, and there was nothing to be afraid of. Nothing at all.

Eventually, she conjured up enough courage to stand up, get dressed, and face the day. The first day of her new life living on the Flats family farm out in the Hill Country.

It turned out to be even weirder than the night before.

LIVING OUTSIDE OF COMFORT

7

When she got downstairs, she found Uncle Roscoe sitting on the couch in his *Star Wars* pajamas, watching cartoons while he ate Fruity Pebbles out of a comically large cereal bowl.

"Good morning, Opal!" he said. "Care for some sugary cereal?"

"I'd love some!" she replied. "But, well…my mama never let me have sugary cereal for breakfast."

He smiled and grabbed another giant bowl, which he filled up with Fruity Pebbles and handed to her.

"You know," he said, pouring her some milk, "your grandma never used to let me and your daddy eat sugary cereal for breakfast, either. But after she went up to heaven, our daddy changed the rules. He told us that from there on out, our mama would've wanted us to eat all the sugary cereal we pleased, especially if it made missing her a little easier on us. And now I'm telling you the same thing."

He smiled and handed her a spoon.

"Thanks, Uncle Roscoe."

"You're welcome, Niece Opal." He raised his cereal bowl and clinked it against hers. "Cheers!"

"Cheers!" she echoed. Then she tried her first spoonful of the multicolored ambrosia he'd placed before her. Her face lit up with surprise.

"Holy cow!" she exclaimed, around a mouthful of cereal. "It's delicious!" Then she began shoveling spoonful after spoonful of Fruity Pebbles into her mouth.

Opal had never tasted anything so good in her entire life. She wolfed down the entire bowl in just a few minutes, then poured herself another one. She gave her uncle a sheepish sideways glance, but he just nodded in approval and handed her the remote control for the television.

"It's Saturday morning!" he said. "That means it's time for Saturday-morning cartoons!" He pointed at the TV screen. "I've already got this episode on tape, so you can put on whatever you want."

He was watching a cartoon she'd never seen before called *Robotech*, which had lots of spaceships and aliens in it. Opal changed the channel and immediately found her favorite cartoon, *Muppet Babies*, which was just beginning. Opal started singing along with the opening theme song, and then Uncle Roscoe started singing it right along with her, while doing a near-perfect imitation of Kermit the Frog's voice.

This had a surprising effect on Opal. It made her laugh. Long and loud. It was the first time she'd laughed since losing her mom. But in that moment, she was too busy laughing to realize it.

They spent the rest of the morning watching cartoons and eating cereal and playing games on Opal's Atari, which her uncle had already hooked up to the big TV in the living room for her.

After lunch, Uncle Roscoe let Opal play a bunch of different computer games on his TRS-80, including one she really liked called *ELIZA* where she was able to say things to the computer by typing them in, and then it would respond to her just like a person would. It even read its responses aloud in a robotic voice. Opal spent over an hour talking to it and asking it questions before the computer began repeating itself and she got bored.

Then her uncle showed her a computer program that he'd created himself called Farm Master that could help farmers figure out when to rotate their crops and calculate how much fertilizer to use and

stuff like that. Opal couldn't believe that her uncle had written the whole program all by himself. She thought it was incredible!

That afternoon they rambled into Comfort to buy groceries. Comfort was the name of the town closest to their farm. On the way, they passed the tiny local middle school Opal knew she'd be attending when she started back in the fall, but she didn't ask her uncle any questions about it. School still seemed like a long way off. She had the whole summer stretched out ahead of her.

On the drive back home, Uncle Roscoe apologized to Opal for living "out in the middle of nowhere." He said their closest neighbors (aside from the bats) were a couple of other farmers who lived miles and miles away. He'd gotten used to no one else being around, but he was worried it might be too lonesome for Opal.

She liked it, though, because it was so peaceful. And she thought the landscape was gorgeous! There were hills and trees every which way she looked. It was the opposite of the flatness and desolation of Level Land. And best of all, there weren't any dust storms or windstorms looming just over the horizon that might suddenly blow you away like a tumbleweed.

At least, that was what Opal believed at the time.

After she helped him put away the groceries, Opal asked Uncle Roscoe if she could also help feed the cows or the chickens. That was when he turned beet red and confessed to her that he didn't *own* any cows or chickens. Not anymore. He'd sold all the animals on the farm to other farmers shortly after he inherited the place.

"I'm just not cut out for animal husbandry," he said. "I don't have the stomach for it."

"What's 'animal husbandry'?" Opal asked.

"It's when you keep a bunch of animals penned up in a corral or locked up in a cage their whole lives, so you can steal all their milk and eggs, day after day, year after year, until you finally decide to kill and eat them. Then you do the same thing all over again to their children."

Opal gave him a horrified look, then shook her head.

"You're right, Uncle Roscoe," she said. "You're definitely not cut out to be a farmer."

"Tell the truth and shame the devil!" he replied, laughing. "You know, I made the mistake of sharing my opinions on livestock with your grandpa Filo one time, when I was about your age, and he nearly disowned me." He shrugged and tipped his hat up. "But after he left this place to me, I decided I'd stick to growing vegetables. Unfortunately, I'm not very good at that, either. But I make ends meet. Sort of. Okay, not really. At all."

He laughed again, but Opal could tell he was only half joking. She thought about those past-due bills he'd stuffed in the glove box but decided not to mention them. Instead, she began to walk from room to room, looking at all the black-and-white family photos hanging on every single wall of the house. Many of them appeared to have been hung in chronological order, so as Opal looked over them, it was almost like a time-lapse film of her grandparents growing old and her father and uncle growing up. She was beginning to understand why her uncle still couldn't let go of this place. It was all he had left of his parents and his big brother, and he wanted to hold on tight to his memories of them as long as he possibly could. As long as he stayed here, he would be surrounded by them.

Opal knew exactly how he felt. But, thanks to a whole lot of different song lyrics, like the ones Paul McCartney wrote for "Yesterday," she also knew that holding on too tight to the past for too long could be really bad for you, even if it felt really good while you were doing it. Especially if you were doing it to avoid dealing with the present. Or facing your future.

THE CLOTHESLINE CREW

Later that same evening, when the sun started to get low in the sky, Uncle Roscoe asked Opal if she'd changed her mind about hiking over to the big old beautiful cave to watch the bats fly out for the night. To his surprise, Opal said yes. She wasn't sure why, but now she was eager to see the bats and their home. She asked her uncle how far away the cave was; he said it was only about a mile, just over the hill in the distance, beyond the edge of their property.

On the way there, they walked across the empty field of grass adjacent to the house, passing directly under the spot where Opal had seen the flying saucer hovering the night before. She scanned the entire area, but there didn't appear to be any trace of it left behind. No marks or burns or crop circles. Nothing. Maybe that was because the thing had never actually landed....

Yeah, Opal thought. *Or maybe it's because you dreamed the whole thing up.*

They reached the big old beautiful cave right at sunset, just in time to see the first few bats flutter out of the cave. Then they saw them circle around and fly right back into it again.

"Those were the scouts," Uncle Roscoe explained. "They fly out first, before the rest of the colony, to check the temperature, see if it's raining, and make sure there aren't any mean old hawks or owls waiting around to ambush everyone. Then the scouts fly back inside and let the rest of the colony know if the coast is clear."

Opal figured it must be clear tonight, because a few seconds later, thousands and thousands of bats began to pour out of the mouth of the cave, flapping and fluttering up into the night sky in one giant undulating stream of squeaking and chittering critters, all silhouetted against the blazing orange-and-violet sunset.

The sight affected Opal in a way she didn't expect. It was one of the most beautiful and profound things she'd ever seen. She'd had a giant hole in her heart ever since her mama died, and this was the first thing to make her feel like it might be starting to heal. For some reason, she suddenly felt a deep psychic connection to all those furry little flying critters zooming up overhead. It was almost as if she could think what they were thinking and feel what the bats were feeling. And right at that moment, they were all feeling mighty hungry.

Out of nowhere, Opal's stomach let out a long, slow growl. It was loud enough for Uncle Roscoe to hear it.

"Whoa!" he said. "Are you hungry, kiddo?"

"Yeah," she replied, trying to calm her stomach. "I'm starving all of a sudden."

"Well, we can't have that!" he said, turning to lead her back toward home. "It's taco night! And we've got all the fixings back at the house ready to go."

"I love tacos!" Opal declared.

"So do I!" her uncle replied. "And you want to hear some more good news?"

"Yes! Please!"

"It also happens to be Saturday night," he said. "And that means the best program in the history of television will be on later. And we're gonna watch it! While we eat a mountain of tacos and drink a gallon of sweet tea."

Opal was intrigued but not yet convinced.

"What is this program called?" she asked.

"*Austin City Limits!*" he replied. "It's my all-time favorite show, and they record it in my all-time favorite town. Austin! I think it's gonna be right up your alley, Opal."

Opal suddenly felt a big lump rising in her throat, because she had seen *Austin City Limits* before, a bunch of times. Her mama used to let her stay up late and watch it with her sometimes, if there was a guest on they both really liked. In fact, *Austin City Limits* was probably the one TV show that Opal associated with her mama the most. Just hearing the name of the show triggered a flood of memories that nearly brought Opal to tears. But she held them back. She didn't want Uncle Roscoe to feel bad for putting the show on. And now she found herself desperately wanting to watch it, even if it did remind her of how much she missed her mama. So she kept quiet and pretended as if she'd never seen it before.

"Why do you think I'll like it?" she asked her uncle.

"Because it's a show where all the best musicians in the world show up and play all their best music!"

"You're right, Uncle Roscoe," she replied. "That does sound right up my alley."

Austin City Limits was a live music program on PBS, broadcast from a little building on the University of Texas campus over in Austin. Different musicians and bands appeared on the show every week. That evening the musical guest was Ray Charles! With the Raelettes and the Ray Charles Orchestra! They put on an incredible show, and Opal thought it was over way too soon. She craved more live music! Luckily, it turned out that Uncle Roscoe had recorded a whole bunch of past *ACL* episodes on videotape. He and Opal started watching them, one after another. She couldn't get enough. Most of them were older episodes that she'd never seen before. A few of them were more recent episodes that she'd already seen with her mama, like the one with Tom Waits, but she didn't mind watching them again. Uncle Roscoe really got into the music, and he knew all sorts of interesting facts and trivia about the musicians that he shared with her during each show.

Ray Charles, the best piano player of all time. Favorite songs: "Mess Around" and "Hit the Road Jack."

When Leo Kottke plays his twelve-string guitar, he makes it sound like four different people playing four different guitars at once. He also writes great songs and sings them in his real deep voice. It's a great combination.

Halfway through the Leo Kottke episode, while he was performing a song that Opal really liked called "Jack Gets Up," Opal suddenly had a strange sensation, like someone was watching her. She felt the hairs on the back of her neck stand up. She glanced over at Uncle Roscoe, but he was staring at the TV and grooving to the music.

Opal slowly turned around, and through the large open window behind her, she saw something she couldn't quite believe—a row of bats hanging upside down from the clothesline in the backyard. They were only a few feet away from the window, so they had a perfect view of the television. There were about a dozen of them, and they were all just hanging there, staring intently at the TV screen. And Opal could swear that a few of them were bobbing their heads up and down slightly in time with the music. Opal didn't know how, but she could tell the bats were really enjoying it.

She tapped Uncle Roscoe on the shoulder and pointed out the window.

"Looks like a few friends dropped in to watch the show with us," she said.

When Uncle Roscoe turned around and saw the bats, he literally fell out of his chair. Opal helped him get to his feet.

"Whoa!" he said, blinking his eyes repeatedly in shock. "I've never seen bats hang on that clothesline before. Ever!"

Opal nodded, then shrugged. "Well, I guess there's a first time for everything."

She studied the bats in silence for a moment, then she walked over to the big Philco television and turned the volume knob up as far as it would go, so the bats could hear better.

Uncle Roscoe smiled and nodded his approval, then he ran around and opened up all the other windows in the living room, too. The sound of Leo Kottke's twelve-string guitar began to drift outside and echo across the backyard. Opal sensed that the increase in the music's volume made the bats very happy. They all began to chitter loudly and flutter their wings in a show of gratitude.

Opal walked over to the window to get a closer look at them. When she got within a few yards of the clothesline, she suddenly discovered that she was able to understand everything the bats were saying to one another. In her head, all their chittering and squeaking made perfect sense, like they were speaking in plain English. It was like she could read their thoughts.

She wondered how this could be possible. Then she remembered her strange encounter the night before. Had that flying saucer she'd seen done something to her? It must have. Either that, or she was losing her marbles.

She stood there and listened to the bats as they talked excitedly among themselves about the music they were hearing. Apparently, none of them had ever heard music before tonight, and now that they had, they all found themselves irresistibly drawn to its source, as if they were hypnotized by the melody. Each new song they heard seemed to put them into an even deeper state of auditory ecstasy.

When one of the bats heard a song they really loved, a powerful feeling would suddenly come over them, and they wouldn't be able to help themselves.

They'd have to fly up and dance along with the music in the sky, flapping their tiny wings in time to the rhythm as they cartwheeled through the air.

That's when Opal had a stunning realization... these bats were all melomaniacs, just like her! Their intense connection to the music seemed so powerful it was almost supernatural.

Opal wondered if the bats' extrasensitive hearing allowed them to appreciate music in ways that human beings couldn't, because their ears could hear it more clearly and at many different frequencies. The sound of music seemed to make the bats feel euphoric, which in turn caused them to create a new kind of music of their own. They would "sing along" by emitting a low-frequency humming sound, sort of like a cat purring, and when Opal heard it for the first time, it made her feel euphoric, too, and she found herself enjoying the music even more— something she didn't even know was possible.

Somehow, listening to a song with one of these bats nearby could make its melody sound even sweeter.

Opal decided to call the bats' strange music-enhancing ability their "mojo," after she saw all of them dancing and humming along to one of her favorite songs, "Got My Mojo Working" by Muddy Waters. *Mojo* was another word for magic, and that's exactly what the sound the bats were making felt like to Opal. Some kind of musical magic that made anyone who heard it enjoy the music even more.

When Uncle Roscoe joined her at the window and he got his first earful of the bats' mojo, too, Opal could tell it had the same euphoric effect on him. For the next few minutes they both just stood there at the window together, grooving to the music and basking in the mojo that all twelve of the bats hanging on their clothesline were putting out.

"I've decided to give our new melomaniac bat friends a nickname," Opal declared, reaching both of her arms out toward the bats. "The Clothesline Crew!"

As soon as she said it, the bats all began to chitter and flutter their wings excitedly.

"I think they like it!" Uncle Roscoe said, turning to Opal. "And I like it, too! Let's make their new nickname official. A toast!"

He raised his glass of sweet tea to the bats. Then he cleared his throat and waited until Opal raised hers, too.

"To our new melomaniac bat friends!" he said. "The Clothesline Crew!"

The bats chittered and fluttered their wings again. She could sense that they really liked their new nickname. And that they really liked Opal and Uncle Roscoe, too. She could feel them beaming gratitude back at them both, and Opal did her best to beam it right back at them.

And that was how their friendship began.

Opal and Uncle Roscoe started to leave all their living room windows open on Saturday nights to give the Clothesline Crew a better view of their TV, and to allow their mojo to drift all through the house.

Opal would always turn the volume up real high to make sure the bats could hear the music, too. But after a few weeks, Uncle Roscoe decided that wasn't good enough, so he hooked the TV up to his stereo and placed its speakers over by the window facing the clothesline, so their furry flying friends could hear the music even better.

Their hospitality had the intended effect. The bats kept on coming back. Every Saturday night, instead of flying out to hunt for bugs with everyone else, the Clothesline Crew would fly over to the Flats family farm to hang upside down on their clothesline in pairs and watch their favorite show along with them. Even though they left their windows open for hours, no bugs ever flew into the house, because none of them ever made it past the bats.

After a while, Uncle Roscoe started bringing the small color TV in his bedroom down so he could set it up outside and give the bats the best *ACL* viewing experience possible. He placed a metal ladder right beside the clothesline and then rested the TV set on its little foldout paint-pail shelf. Opal suggested that he trying turning the TV upside down, so that the screen would look right side up to the bats. When Uncle Roscoe did this, the Clothesline Crew nearly lost their collective bat minds, squeaking and flapping their wings and swinging their pointy little tails around. Opal figured the bats liked this new setup so much because it made all the musicians on the TV look as if they were hanging upside down by their feet, too.

Before long, Saturday nights weren't enough for them, and the bats started showing up on Friday and Sunday nights as well. So Opal and Uncle Roscoe would throw open their windows on those nights, too, and then put on a tape of old *ACL* episodes to watch with their bat friends.

Sometimes, when the evening's episode of *Austin City Limits* was over and Uncle Roscoe shut off the TV, the Clothesline Crew wouldn't leave. They would just keep on hanging there, looking forlorn and pining away for more music. So Uncle Roscoe would put some more music on for them, blasting the radio out over the fields from the big stereo speakers he set up by the window. And as they listened to the music, the Clothesline Crew would fly out over those same fields and gobble up all the bugs that were eating away at Uncle Roscoe's crops. It was the bats' way of saying thank you to the Flats family for sharing their love of music with them.

At the end of each Sunday night, Opal would

always wave goodbye to the Clothesline Crew as they flew off, shouting, "We'll see y'all next weekend!"

And they would. The bats reappeared on their clothesline every Friday, Saturday, and Sunday night, week after week, without fail. Opal and Uncle Roscoe would look forward to seeing their furry little bat friends all week long.

As time went on, Opal began to notice strange quirks in their behavior. For example, the bats in the Clothesline Crew usually preferred to hang side by side on the clothesline in pairs of two, and each pair favored a different genre of music. It was easy to tell which bats were enjoying a song the most, because they were the ones putting out the most mojo while it was being played.

Opal decided she should probably give each of the twelve bats a nickname, to make it easier to tell them apart. She knew all of them already had names in their own squeaky bat language. But she didn't know what they were, and even if she had, she couldn't have pronounced them. So she gave each of the bats a nickname that she *could* pronounce.

Uncle Roscoe had an old street map of Austin

pinned to the wall, and it gave Opal a bolt of inspiration. Since her new bat friends loved *Austin City Limits* so much, she decided to name each one of them after a street in downtown Austin.

As she studied the street map, the perfect name for each member of the Clothesline Crew seemed to leap out at her. Opal pointed to each pair of bats and announced their new nicknames in a loud voice, so both they and Uncle Roscoe could hear.

Pearl & Sabine were best friends who loved rhythm and blues music.

Trinity & Colorado both adored country music. They also loved cowboy movies! Sometimes the two of them would show up at the farm again on random weeknights as well, to hang on the clothesline and watch old westerns on TV over Uncle Roscoe's shoulder.

Cesar & Jacinto were brothers who were both wild about Tejano music.

Koenig & Lamar loved grooving to rap, hip-hop, and funk music.

Rainey & Red both preferred to get down to good old-fashioned rock and roll. They dug hard rock, punk rock, and rockabilly. Anything that rocked!

The last two bats in the Clothesline Crew were Opal's favorites, because she sensed they were a lot like her. They both loved *all* kinds of music, and they couldn't resist dancing to just about any song they heard. One was female, and the other was male. She decided to call them **Lavaca & Brazos**.

Lavaca and Brazos weren't a matched pair like the others. They both liked to fly solo. They also liked to dance solo and hang upside down from the clothesline solo, too. Opal sensed a lot of tension between Lavaca and Brazos. She also got the impression that their shared love of music was just about the only thing the two of them had in common.

Lavaca was a serious and hardworking bat, and an upstanding member of the colony. She volunteered to teach younger bat pups how to fly and echolocate. Lavaca liked to obey the rules and got

annoyed when other bats didn't. That was why Brazos's behavior really stuck in her craw.

Brazos wasn't the least bit serious, and no one would have ever accused him of being hardworking. Most of the other bats, including Lavaca, thought he was a lazy slacker, and he didn't deny it. When Brazos wasn't goofing off, he was usually showing off. He also liked to sleep a lot, and he had a bad habit of showing up late for everything, including dinner. Worst of all, sometimes Brazos even refused to obey the basic unspoken rules of being a bat.

For example, when all the other bats flew off out

of the big old beautiful cave each night at sunset, they would fly to the south. Everyone *always* exited to the south, every evening. Except Brazos. He always flew off in some other direction, just to be different. He fancied himself to be some sort of rebel. And maybe he was, too.

One thing was for sure, though. Lavaca and Brazos both adored music as much as any creature alive, and the two of them had more mojo than all the other members of the Clothesline Crew combined, which was saying something.

After a few weeks of reading their minds and

eavesdropping on their squeaky little conversations, Opal learned that the twelve members of the Clothesline Crew had something else in common, in addition to their shared loved of music. All of them were orphans, too. They'd each lost both of their parents to predators, accidents, or illness. And the mutual loss they'd each suffered was also what had originally bonded all of them together into a group. The twelve of them had formed a new family, made up of bats who'd all lost their original ones.

And now, in a weird way, Opal and Uncle Roscoe had become part of that family of misfit melomaniac orphans, too.

Opal figured that must be why she felt so connected to these creatures. All of them were grieving from a terrible loss, just like her. And just like her, all of them were trying to heal their broken hearts with music.

And Opal sensed that it was working. For all of them, including her.

Thanks to her strange new friendship with the Clothesline Crew, and the help of sweet Uncle Roscoe, Opal was starting to feel something she was worried she might never be able to feel again. True happiness.

Opal still missed her mama something fierce, and she knew she always would. But with each passing day, the pain of losing her was a little easier for Opal to bear. And as a result, the music she heard each day seemed to sound just a little bit sweeter.

Things were beginning to look up. And then everything came crashing down.

BULLDOZERS AND DYNAMITE

That morning, the sun rose over the big old beautiful cave for what would be the very last time. But none of the bats knew that yet. The entire colony was sound asleep, including Lavaca and Brazos and the rest of the Clothesline Crew. So you can imagine how scary it was for all of them to be woken up by the sound of a huge explosion. A million pairs of supersensitive bat ears suddenly heard a deafening BOOM that shook the entire cave!

That boom was followed by several more— a series of even louder booms that came in rapid succession. The roof of the big old beautiful cave continued to shake and tremble, as if they were experiencing some sort of apocalyptic earthquake. The bats were all terrified, young and old alike. None of them understood what was happening, because nothing like this had ever happened before. But they all sensed instinctively that it wasn't safe for any of them to remain inside their cave a moment longer. They needed to get outside, right now.

The bat parents scooped up their bat pups, and every last bat in the entire colony hightailed it out of there, flying up out of the mouth of the cave as fast as their little wings would carry them, fleeing for their lives from the only home any of them had ever known.

Thankfully, the entire colony managed to escape out of the mouth of the cave and make it to safety up in the sky. Once they were all circling high above it, the bats all gazed back down at their home in horror, because now they could see that it was surrounded by humans. Humans with giant yellow machines. And like many other members of the animal kingdom, the bats knew this was a deadly combination.

These weren't friendly humans, like Opal and

her uncle. They were mean-spirited men in hard hats with no regard for the natural world. Each one was operating a mechanized yellow monster called a bulldozer, or an earthmover, or a wrecking ball. And every one of them had the name *Muckerno Limestone* stenciled across its metal skin.

These instruments of destruction were demolishing everything in their path, knocking down trees and tearing up the beautiful hilly countryside.

The mean-spirited men in hard hats had also brought along something else. Something even worse than their monstrous yellow machines.

An explosive called dynamite.

That was what they were using to blow up the big old beautiful cave and everything around it, with one devastating explosion after another. That was the source of all the shaking and booming that had driven the bats out of their home.

The humans were destroying the big old beautiful cave and everything around it so they could dig a massive hole in the ground called a quarry, where they could carve out giant blocks of limestone and truck them off to sell to other humans. Humans used

limestone to build their buildings, and they were always building more buildings, so they needed a steady supply of limestone. And they didn't much care where they got it or who was in the way.

They didn't care about the big old beautiful cave, or the bats who lived inside it. They didn't care about the rolling green forest, or the birds and squirrels and deer and coyotes and countless other little critters who called it home. According to the big, important human plans they'd cooked up, all that natural beauty was just standing in their way, so one day they'd up and decided to destroy it. And that day was today.

As the terrified bats continued to circle up above, they heard another rapid series of booming explosions from somewhere down below, followed by a roar of rocky rumbling that sounded like an avalanche. The bats all turned to look back down at the mouth of their cave, just in time to see its roof collapse.

The bats couldn't believe their horrified little eyes. They didn't think this was possible. Their big old beautiful cave had just caved in!

Their home had just been destroyed forever, right in front of them.

The bats didn't know what to do. There were nearly a million of them. And they were all suddenly homeless.

Brazos was a very deep sleeper, and he was always disoriented for a few minutes after he woke up, so he was one of the last bats to escape from the cave that morning.

Brazos flew north as he exited, in the opposite

direction as everyone else. As he did, he happened to fly past one of the giant bulldozers lumbering through the nearby forest. The man operating the bulldozer was listening to a giant portable radio, and at that moment it happened to be playing a song Brazos recognized: "You're Gonna Miss Me" by the 13th Floor Elevators. Uncle Roscoe had played it for the Clothesline Crew a bunch of times because they all seemed to like it so much.

Brazos used to love that song, but now he knew it had been ruined for him forever, because for the rest of his life, whenever he heard it, it would always remind him of this terrible day of bulldozers, dynamite, and destruction.

The bats continued to circle high overhead, waiting for it all to end. But the humans didn't stop once they'd destroyed the big old beautiful cave. They were just getting started. They kept right on blasting massive holes in the earth, all day long. And each explosion sounded like the end of the world. Because it was.

Eventually their tiny ears and hearts couldn't stand it anymore, and the bats all flew away from there as fast as their wings would carry them.

The colony quickly realized that they didn't have anywhere to go now. They no longer had anywhere to live or to sleep or to nurse their newborn pups. And to make matters even worse, there were dark clouds gathering on the horizon. A nasty Hill Country thunderstorm was rolling in. The bats all knew instinctively that a whole lot of rain and lightning and thunder was headed their way.

They sent out all their best scouts, and they

flew for miles in every direction, searching for a new home for their homeless colony. But most of the caves they found weren't big enough, and the rest were already occupied by another bat colony, by other animals, or by more humans who were engaged in another mining operation.

Meanwhile, the sky continued to darken. Then rain began to pour down so hard that the poor homeless bats were finally forced to roost in a stand of old trees, which didn't provide much shelter from the horrendous storm. Everyone's fur got soaking wet.

The colony huddled as closely together as they

could, to try to stay warm by sharing their body heat. None of them knew what else to do, or where else to go.

Brazos couldn't bear to see his friends and family in so much suffering. And he knew that when night fell, the temperature would drop drastically, and before long the newborn bat pups would be cold and shivering in their wet fur. The elderly bats would be freezing cold, too.

He could still hear the words of that song echoing in his head. *You're gonna miss me, baby!*

Brazos already missed the big old beautiful cave. He missed their home. But that home no longer existed, and he knew the colony had to find a new one. As soon as possible. In the meantime, they needed to find a place where they could get out of the rain. But where were a million homeless bats supposed to find shelter?

The words of the song echoed in his head again, and this time they made Brazos think of his two friends over on the Flats family farm. Opal and Roscoe. Maybe they would help?

Considering what all those humans had just done to his family, the notion of going to some other humans to ask for help didn't exactly seem like the brightest idea. But it was the only one he had, so he shared it with Lavaca and the other members of the Clothesline Crew. They all agreed that Opal and her uncle were different. They weren't like the mean-spirited men in hard hats who had just destroyed their home. Opal and her uncle were kind and good and would help them if they could. Everyone in the Clothesline Crew felt certain of it.

The twelve of them decided to leave the rest of the colony and fly over to the Flats farm, to see if their human friends would help them.

What they didn't know was that Opal and Uncle Roscoe were in the process of losing their home, too.

10

FOREGONE FORECLOSURE

Opal was having a terrible nightmare, about an earthquake striking the big old beautiful cave while she was inside it, visiting with her friends in the Clothesline Crew. She was hanging upside down from the roof of the cave by her toes, like they were. But the cave was starting to tremble and collapse, so all the bats began to fly outside. Opal tried to follow them, but she wasn't a bat, so when she unclenched her toes, instead of taking flight she just began to fall, plunging into a darkened abyss down below, as the rest of the cave continued to collapse on top of her.

That was when she finally woke up in her bed

with a shriek, reflexively shielding her head with both her arms.

She leaped out of the bed and then began to back slowly away from it, as if the thing might be radioactive or cursed or both. She'd never in her life had a dream like that. She'd felt like she was really there, and like it was all really happening.

Then she had a terrible thought. What if it really was? What if that wasn't a nightmare she'd been having, but some kind of vision of the future?

She got dressed as quickly as she could, then hurried downstairs to tell Uncle Roscoe about the nightmare. But when she found him, she suddenly forgot all about it.

He was sitting at the kitchen table, clutching a crumpled piece of paper with the words *NOTICE OF IMPENDING FORECLOSURE* printed across the top in big red letters, followed by a bunch of fine print in black. He was staring at it so intently he didn't even notice when Opal walked in behind him, or when she began to read over his shoulder. When she finally cleared her throat to say good morning, it startled him so badly he literally fell right out of his chair.

"Whoa!" he shouted, laughing as he picked himself back up. Then he pointed a finger at Opal. "You snuck up on me! Like some sort of ninja!"

"Sorry," she replied. "I didn't mean to." She pointed at the paper in his hands. "That looks like bad news."

He frowned at her in silence for a moment, then nodded.

"Well, it isn't good news," he said. "That's for sure."

He motioned to the empty chair across from him, and Opal took a seat. He poured her a big bowl of Fruity Pebbles and another for himself, then passed her the milk.

"Thank you," she said.

"You're welcome."

He opened his mouth to speak a few times, but no words came out. Opal could see how worried and upset he was, and how hard he was trying to hide it. She knew exactly how he felt because she was trying to hide how worried and upset she was, too. She'd just lost her home up in Lubbock, and now it looked liked she was gonna lose this one.

She felt like bawling her fool head off, but she didn't want to make Uncle Roscoe feel even worse. So instead she reached out and placed her hand on his arm.

"Just give it to me straight, Uncle Roscoe," Opal said. "I can handle it."

He gave her a surprised look, then nodded and took a deep breath.

"I'm sorry, Opal," he said. "I really screwed up pretty bad. I got too far behind on the mortgage payments for this farm, and now the bank has decided to foreclose on it. That means they're taking this place away from me, and as of this Friday, I won't own it anymore. The bank will. And they want us to move out by the end of the month. So we're gonna have to find us a new place to live. But don't you worry, now—I'm already formulating a plan. I got an offer to sell the rights to my Farm Master program a while back, and I'm gonna take it. And the local RadioShack has been trying to hire me forever, full-time with benefits, so—"

"Is this happening because you took me in?" Opal asked, interrupting him.

"Oh, of course not, honey!" he replied emphatically. "I fell behind on the mortgage payments long before you got here. This farm has been losing money since before my daddy passed." He threw up his hands. "This is happening because I'm a rotten farmer! And a stubborn idiot to boot!" He shook his head. "Why did I hold on to this place when I knew the bank was just gonna foreclose on it? Why didn't I just sell it to Muckerno Limestone when I had the chance?"

"Because you're a good person, Uncle Roscoe," Opal said, resting a hand on his shoulder. "That's why! You held on to this place for your mama and your daddy, and for my daddy, too, because you loved them and missed them all so much, and you wanted to honor them by preserving the home you all shared."

Uncle Roscoe tried to respond, but he was too choked up, so Opal just squeezed his arm and kept on talking.

"And you didn't sell this land to Muckerno Limestone because you knew they were planning to destroy it," she reminded him. "And taking their money would have made you a part of it. You couldn't let that happen, and you didn't." She smiled at him. "You did the right thing, Uncle Roscoe. I'm so proud of you."

She gave him a big bear hug. He hugged her back, just as tight.

"Thank you for saying all that," he said. "I was worried you were gonna be mad at me. For failing to provide you with a stable home environment."

She shook her head and smiled at him.

"Remember what you told me?" she said. "We're family. That means we stick together, right? Through thick and thin, frown or grin..."

"Until we win," he added half-heartedly.

"Exactly!" she replied. "But with slightly more enthusiasm."

"I'm afraid we can't win this one, kiddo," he said, gazing forlornly out the kitchen window. "The bank is already planning to sell this farm to Muckerno Limestone after they foreclose. Muckerno already bought up all the land around us, and before long they'll be blasting this place to pieces to dig their accursed quarry...."

Opal immediately flashed back to the hauntingly real nightmare she'd awoken from earlier that morning, and the terrifying feeling of the big old beautiful cave collapsing down on her.

Now she felt certain of it. That wasn't a nightmare she'd had. It was a premonition.

She ran into the living room and pressed her face up against the window that overlooked the clothesline. It was empty, of course. It was still daytime. The bats should all be asleep right now. But something told her they weren't sleeping. She sensed they were all wide awake. And in deep distress.

In the distance, she could see a giant mass of dark storm clouds gathering on the horizon. She took them as another sign. Something was terribly wrong.

"Uncle Roscoe!" Opal called over her shoulder, in a voice suddenly filled with fear. "I think something terrible is going to happen to the bats, if it hasn't already!"

"Why would you say that?" he replied, hurrying to join her at the window. "I'm sure they're all fine, honey. Safe and sound in their cave."

Opal shook her head.

"No," she said, turning to face him. "They're in trouble. I had a nightmare about their cave collapsing. But it didn't feel like a nightmare. It felt real. Would you please go check on them for me, Uncle Roscoe? Please?"

He studied her face for a few seconds, then nodded and put on his raincoat.

"Don't you want to come with me?" he asked.

She began to nod, then shook her head.

"I don't think I should," she said. "I'm not sure I can bear to see it. Besides, I want to stay here, in case the bats come to us looking for help."

She glanced back out the window at the empty clothesline.

"Okay," he said, opening the front door. "Stay right here. I'll be back in a flash. And try to stay positive."

She nodded and gave him a thumbs-up. He gave her one back, and then he departed, closing and locking the door behind him.

Her uncle had been gone only a few minutes when the sky outside suddenly darkened, and the biggest, loudest, nastiest thunderstorm Opal had ever seen descended on the farm, like the righteous wrath of Mother Nature had suddenly been unleashed from the heavens. Rain was falling in sheets as thick as lead, while crooked tines of lightning arced across the rumbling sky and waves of rolling thunder rattled the windows of the old farmhouse.

She suddenly felt awful for sending Uncle Roscoe out into that mess. She really hoped the bats weren't out in it, too. It must be pretty difficult for them to fly when it was raining this hard.

She glanced back out the window and jumped in surprise, because all twelve members of the Clothesline Crew were hanging there on the clothesline just a few feet away, out in the middle of all that pouring rain and lightning and thunder. It was like they'd appeared out of nowhere.

She opened the window and locked eyes with Brazos, and in that instant, she knew everything that had happened to him that day—as if his recent memories had been transferred directly to her.

Opal let out an involuntary scream, as she relived the terrible events at the cave earlier that morning through Brazos's eyes and ears, experiencing it all in the span of a few seconds. She heard the deafening detonations of the dynamite, each amplified a thousand times by his supersensitive bat hearing. She felt the terrible tremors as they rumbled through the rocky roof of the cave through her clawed bat feet as she clung to its underside. It was just like her nightmare earlier that morning, except this time she *did* have wings, and instead of falling, she took flight and zoomed down and out of the mouth of the collapsing cave faster than a...well, faster than a bat out of you-know-where! Because that's exactly what Brazos felt like in that moment, as he barely escaped his home, only to witness its collapse and annihilation a few seconds later, with the song "You're Gonna Miss Me" still ringing in his—and now Opal's—tiny little ears...

The sudden sound of the front door blowing in and slamming against the doorjamb startled Opal and broke off her psychic communion with Brazos.

She looked over to see Uncle Roscoe standing in the open doorway in his dripping raincoat, with an extremely worried look on his face.

"Opal, are you okay?" he asked. "I thought I heard you screaming."

She wiped at the tears streaming down her face. She was still too traumatized by what she'd just seen to form words. Instead she simply pointed out the window. Uncle Roscoe turned to see all twelve members of the Clothesline Crew staring back at him. Lightning would flash every few seconds, briefly illuminating all their sad little faces. They looked utterly despondent hanging out there on the clothesline in the pouring rain. But Uncle Roscoe smiled when he saw them and let out a long sigh of relief.

"Thank heavens those little guys are okay," he said, before his expression immediately darkened again. "I'm worried about the rest of their colony, though."

He closed the door behind him and shrugged off his raincoat, then hurried over to Opal. He felt her forehead, then knelt down in front of her to examine her complexion.

"Do you feel all right?" he asked, standing back up. "You look really pale. Did the Clothesline Crew scare you when you spotted them out there?"

Opal shook her head. Then she took a deep breath and slowly exhaled it in an attempt to calm herself down. It helped, so she did it a few more times, until she finally felt in control of her faculties again.

"It's the cave, Uncle Roscoe," she said, holding back sobs. "A bunch of mean-spirited men showed up this morning to destroy it with bulldozers and dynamite! They blasted the big old beautiful cave to pieces. It's gone forever! And now all the bats are homeless. Just like us."

Uncle Roscoe stared at her in disbelief. Then he slowly nodded.

"You're right," he said. "About the cave. Those were Muckerno Limestone's bulldozers. They sent in a whole demolition crew, and they did what they do. Demolish everything." He glanced over at the bats, then back at her. "But how did you know all of that, Opal?"

She considered telling him the truth—that after

seeing a flying saucer, she'd formed some sort of telepathic link with the bats that allowed her to read their minds and feel their feelings. But she didn't want to make him any more worried about her than he already was, so she ignored his question and told him a few more things that it was impossible for her to know.

"The rest of the colony is somewhere nearby," she said. "Riding out the storm by roosting in some old trees for cover. But they're wet and cold, and they're gonna get even colder tonight. We've got to do something to help them, Uncle Roscoe."

He stared at her in consternation for a few seconds. Then he nodded and looked back out the window. He studied the bats hanging from the clothesline for a moment, then turned back to Opal.

"Get your raincoat and follow me," he said. "I've got an idea."

Opal and Uncle Roscoe ran out into the pouring rain and made their way over to the barn, stomping through giant muddy puddles the whole way. Once they were inside, they began to execute Uncle Roscoe's plan, by stringing up a whole bunch of clotheslines. They put up dozens and dozens of them, running from one end of the barn all the way to the other. These clotheslines created a makeshift roost, where hundreds and hundreds of bats could hang upside down and sleep in safety, out of the torrential rain and the freezing wind.

Opal asked her uncle to string the clotheslines even closer together, because the bats liked to snuggle up side by side to keep one another warm. He didn't question her. He just started stringing the clotheslines closer together like she'd asked. He could obviously see that she had some sort of connection with the bats without her having to explain it. So she decided there was no point in trying to conceal it from him. Uncle Roscoe trusted her, so it only made sense for her to trust him back.

Once they finished preparing the barn, Opal whistled to the Clothesline Crew and all twelve of them immediately flew right over to her like trained pets. They hung upside down from the clothesline directly in front of her as she addressed them, like a general addressing her troops.

"Okay, the barn is finally ready!" she told them. "You should all fly out to the rest of the colony and bring back as many of the youngest and oldest bats as possible, to get them out of the storm for the night. And keep on bringing them until this barn is completely full! Understand?"

The bats all nodded their little heads up and down. Or rather, down and up.

"Okay, then off you go!" Opal shouted. "Please be careful out there!"

In unison, the Clothesline Crew flew off into the rain, as if they'd understood exactly what Opal had said to them.

Uncle Roscoe watched all of this in awe. But he didn't speak, because he didn't know what to say. He couldn't believe his own eyes. He'd known these bats his entire life, but this was the first time he'd ever seen them take commands from someone, as if they'd all been trained in the circus.

Opal and Uncle Roscoe strung up more

clotheslines while they waited. About half an hour later, the Clothesline Crew returned, accompanied by several thousand of their friends—all the oldest and youngest bats in the colony. They filled that barn up all the way to the rafters in a matter of minutes, packing themselves in there like sardines.

When they ran out of room in the barn, Uncle Roscoe ran up to the farmhouse's attic and threw open all its windows. Then he began to string clotheslines across it, too, so that a few hundred more bats could take shelter in there. Then he and

Opal did the same thing inside the garage and then in the old chicken coop and then on the house's front porch. They sheltered bats in every single dry place they could find, except for inside the house. And when there was nowhere else left, they started stringing up clotheslines in the living room and the kitchen, too.

By the time night fell, they had thousands and thousands of bat guests sheltering all over their farm. But Opal and her uncle had still been able to make enough room to shelter only a small fraction of the colony. Everyone else had to sleep out in the rain and weather the storm.

Opal knew this wasn't a permanent solution. The colony still needed a new place to live. And so did she and Uncle Roscoe.

Opal didn't think this was a coincidence. To her it felt like destiny.

But where were they going to find a new home for a million homeless bats? In a place where Opal and her uncle could live nearby and still visit them?

She glanced up at Lavaca and Brazos and the rest of the Clothesline Crew, who were all now hanging on a clothesline strung across their living room, and the answer suddenly popped into her head. And it must've popped into Uncle Roscoe's head at the same exact moment because he suggested it before she had a chance to.

"Opal," he said. "I believe I've had my fill of living outside of Comfort. I think we should pack up our troubles and move to Austin. You, me, and all these bats." He smiled up at all of them, hanging over their heads. "I have this strange feeling we belong there. All of us."

"So do I!" Opal shouted, throwing her arms around him. "Let's do it!"

Uncle Roscoe was surprised by how quickly Opal made up her mind, but he took it in stride. His niece was full of all sorts of surprises today.

"All right, all right, all right!" he replied. "Just one question: Do you think you can convince all these bats to follow us there?"

"Absolutely!" she replied. "They trust me."

The members of the Clothesline Crew all suddenly began to chitter and squeak at once, flapping their wings as if to signal their agreement. Then all the other bats hanging around in the living room joined in, too, giving rise to a cacophony. It freaked Uncle Roscoe out a little, but he went with it.

"I guess it's settled, then!" he said, raising his voice so Opal could hear him over all the noise. "We'll leave for Austin as soon as we finish packing up and moving out. What do you say?"

Opal raised her arms triumphantly toward the squeaking horde of bats suspended above and all around them.

"I say, 'Look out, Austin!!'" she shouted. "Here we come!"

11

AUSTIN CITY LIMIT

A few days later, after they finished settling their affairs in Comfort, Opal and Uncle Roscoe hit the road again in his old Red Rambler. They both turned around to look back as they rambled away from the Flats family farm for the last time. Opal played "On the Road Again" by Willie Nelson on the tape deck, and they left Comfort behind and headed east on the highway, which carried them even deeper into the Texas Hill Country.

Uncle Roscoe had donated nearly everything he owned (except his computers) to the Goodwill earlier that morning. Now he and Opal had all their remaining worldly possessions piled in the back of the Red Rambler.

They also had about one million furry little friends flying somewhere high overhead, all of them following Opal as if she were some sort of bat pied piper.

They were all hurtling forward into a big old cloud of uncertainty. Opal was more than a little frightened of what the future might hold. But she was more than a little excited by it, too.

Eventually, the sun sank into the road behind them, and darkness quickly descended on the road ahead. Uncle Roscoe switched on his headlights and pressed onward, while Opal kept a steady supply of good music coming from the stereo.

She didn't count the miles or ask her uncle how much farther they had to go, because that would only make the time pass more slowly. She just focused her attention on the music and tried to be patient.

Then, at long last, she noticed a faint orange glow on the horizon up ahead of them. It continued to brighten and widen the closer they got, until it was a bright band of light stretching halfway across the horizon, and Opal knew they had to be approaching a pretty big town. Then the Red Rambler crested a hill and suddenly there it was, the Austin skyline, glittering in the distance like Oz at the end of the yellow-brick road. A second later, she spotted a familiar-looking sign posted alongside the road up ahead.

"Look," she said, pointing it out to her uncle. "The AUSTIN CITY LIMIT sign."

"There it is!" he replied. "We made it, Opal!"

She nodded. Her expression suddenly seemed somber.

"Is it okay if we stop by the sign for a minute?" she asked.

"Sure!" he replied. "It's a pretty scenic view, isn't it?"

He pulled the Red Rambler off the highway and parked it directly in front of the AUSTIN CITY LIMIT sign, illuminating it with his headlights. That was when they were able to see the small cluster of bats flying around the sign in circles. Several of them were also hanging upside down from the bottom of it.

"It's the Clothesline Crew!" Opal shouted. "They recognize the sign."

The bats couldn't read, of course. But they recognized the words written on the sign from the opening of the music show they used to watch at the Flats farm every weekend: *Austin City Limits*!

They recognized the Austin skyline in the

distance, too, because a replica of it served as the stage backdrop on that very same show.

But to Opal's surprise, the bats weren't excited about being here. It was the opposite. That big glowing city skyline in the distance frightened them for some reason. And so now it frightened her a little, too.

She had thought Lavaca and Brazos and the rest of the Clothesline Crew would be overjoyed about reaching Austin. They had flown so far, through the lightning and the rain, and now she and Uncle Roscoe had led them to the promised land! The city where all those amazing musicians they adored came to perform their music, week after week!

But the bats weren't thinking about music. They had other concerns.

"What's wrong, Opal?" Uncle Roscoe asked, pointing at her forehead. "You got a furrow in your brow, and I don't know how."

"I think the city looks a lot bigger than they thought it would," she said. "They don't want to go any farther."

Opal and her uncle both climbed out of the

Rambler and walked over to the sign and the bats circling it. When Opal got close enough to read their minds a little more clearly, she finally understood why the Clothesline Crew was so upset.

"They're afraid to follow us into the city," she said. "Because it's a city filled with humans. And humans just destroyed their home and ruined their lives."

"They've got a point," Uncle Roscoe replied. "If I was in their shoes, I'd probably feel the same way." He hunkered down, so that he and Opal were at eye level with each other, then whispered, "What should we say to them, Opal?"

"I'm not sure," she said, biting her lower lip. "I think maybe they want us to convince them that moving their colony here is a good idea."

"Oh yeah?" Uncle Roscoe replied, scratching his chin. "Well, I might be able to do that. Is there any way you can translate what I say to them?"

Opal smiled and shook her head.

"I won't need to translate anything, Uncle Roscoe," she replied. "When we're this close to each other, the bats can read my mind, and I can read theirs. So as long as I can understand what you're saying, the Clothesline Crew will be able to understand it, too. Understand?"

"Not really, no," he said, smiling. "But I defer to you, my dear niece, since I'm still familiarizing myself with the mechanics of interspecies telepathic communication."

Uncle Roscoe stood up straight and turned to address the Clothesline Crew; most of them were still circling overhead.

"Hey, my uncle wants to talk to y'all!" Opal shouted up at them. "Please come on down here for a minute!"

She pointed at a nearby tree branch. In unison, all twelve bats flew over and suspended themselves from it, all hanging side by side in one long row. Once they fell silent, Opal smiled and told her uncle to proceed.

Uncle Roscoe walked over to stand beside the AUSTIN CITY LIMIT sign. Then he cleared his throat and motioned to the glittering city skyline in the distance.

"Welcome, my friends, to Austin!" he shouted. "The Groover's Paradise! You know why folks call it that? Because everyone who lives there loves to groove to music, just like y'all do! There's no other city like it! You're gonna fit right in!" He paused to push his cowboy hat up on his forehead. "And not that bats care about money, but Austin also happens to be an incredibly cheap place to live and an easy place to find work, both factors that will be extremely helpful to us, your human companions, who are pretty broke right now, to be honest."

The bats didn't make a sound. They just stared back at him blankly.

"Did they understand any of that?" Uncle Roscoe asked.

"Yeah," Opal said, nodding. "Every word. You're just not convincing them."

"Really?" Uncle Roscoe asked. "Why not?"

Opal studied the bats in silence for a few seconds before answering.

"Brazos says their colony elders are afraid to go anywhere near such a big human city," Opal told him. "They don't think they'll be welcome there, because most humans are afraid of bats and assume they're all bloodsucking vampires...."

Lavaca let out a long series of soft squeaks and clicking sounds, then jerked her right wing toward the city.

"Lavaca doesn't think this is a good idea, either," Opal said. "She says, 'Austin isn't just *any* human city. It's the state capital! The humans' home base, where they make their stupid human laws!'"

"Lavaca is absolutely right!" Uncle Roscoe said, laughing. "Austin is the state capital. But would you please remind her that Austin is *also* the Live Music Capital of the World? The best place for listening to music on God's green earth!"

He turned to address the bats directly, then pointed toward the city.

"If you move to Austin, you might be taking a risk," he said. "That's true. But while you take it, you'll be listening to all the best musicians making all the best music for all the best people all over town all the dang time!"

The bats studied Uncle Roscoe in silence for

a moment; then they all began to chitter excitedly among themselves. He waited for Opal to translate whatever it was they were saying to one another.

"I think you're starting to win them over, Uncle Roscoe!" she said, listening to the bats intently. "But they're worried that even if they do manage to find a new home somewhere inside the city, humans will just drive them out of it again, like they did before." Opal frowned. "I'm sorry, but I think they were all too traumatized by what happened to the big old beautiful cave to trust humans again. They want to stay as far away from people as possible."

Uncle Roscoe threw up his hands and let out a sigh of frustration.

"They do realize that *you* and *I* are both people," he said. "Don't they?"

"Of course, silly," Opal replied. "But they know we're different."

"Well, that's *exactly* what I've been trying to tell y'all!" he said, spinning on his heel to address the bats once again. "*Everyone in Austin is different, too! The whole crazy town is filled with musicians, slack-ers, hippies, beatniks, outlaws, cosmic cowboys, and misfits of every stripe!" He stretched both of his arms out wide, so that they were level with the city skyline behind him. "Austin is the epicenter of the counterculture! An island of kindness in a sea of narrow-mindedness. It's the only place in this whole stonehearted state where weirdos are welcome! And that's why I believe it will welcome you, too, my furry little friends, if y'all just give it a chance."

Opal broke into applause, and the entire Clothesline Crew immediately joined in, all clapping their tiny wings together in unison. This made a sound that Uncle Roscoe found very disconcerting, and he was relieved when they finally stopped a few seconds later. Then the bats began to chirp and chitter to one another, quietly conferring among themselves. Uncle Roscoe turned to study Opal as she continued to study the bats, waiting for them to make their decision. A few seconds later, Opal suddenly smiled and let out a triumphant "Woo-hoo!"

"You did it, Uncle Roscoe!" she said, throwing her arms around him. "You convinced them to give Austin a chance!"

"Hooray!" he shouted. "They won't regret it!" Then, at a much lower volume, he added, "I hope."

All at once, the bats took flight again. Most of them fluttered off in the direction of the glittering city skyline in the distance, but two of them turned and soared off in the opposite direction.

"Trinity and Colorado are flying back to tell the rest of the colony to stay put for now," Opal explained. "The others are headed into the city to start searching for their new home!"

"Good luck, y'all!" Uncle Roscoe shouted after the Austin-bound bats as they soared out of sight. Then he turned back to Opal. "In the morning, we need to start looking for some new digs, too," he said. "And I also need to find a job or three. It shouldn't be too tough."

Opal suddenly yawned, and that made Uncle Roscoe yawn, too.

"First things first," he said. "We need to get ourselves to a motel to rest up. I know just the place, down on South Congress. You ready to ramble, ace?"

She nodded and took her uncle's hand, and the

two of them walked back to the Red Rambler. As Uncle Roscoe pulled back out onto the highway, they rambled away from the AUSTIN CITY LIMIT sign. As Opal glanced at it in the rearview mirror, a huge smile spread across her face, because she knew what this meant. She was really, truly in Austin now, for the first time ever. The Violet Crown of the Hill Country! The Groover's Paradise! The center of the musical universe!

As they rambled into town in their Red Rambler, Opal rolled down the passenger window, and she was immediately able to hear half a dozen different kinds of music being performed all around her, drifting out in the street through every open window and doorway of every dance hall and honky-tonk they passed along their way. Uncle Roscoe would point and call out the name of each place he recognized as it rolled into view.

"There's Liberty Lunch!" he shouted. "There's La Zona Rosa! That's Strange Brew! And One Knite! And there's the Saxon Pub! That old knight standing guard out front is nicknamed Rusty! Down that way is Threadgill's, where Janis Joplin used to sing. And that little dive over there is the Soap Creek Saloon! Elvis Presley played there, back when it was called the Skyline Club, before anybody had any idea who he was. And it was also the last place Hank Williams ever performed. Right there! And you never know who might be playing there tonight!"

He shook his head and gave his niece a goofy grin.

"There's history everywhere you look in this town," he told her. "Don't you get chills thinking about all the musical legends who have played these clubs and walked these streets? I mean, this is hallowed ground for a couple of melomaniacs like us. Right?"

Opal nodded silently because she was still too overwhelmed by her surroundings to speak. She was realizing that she'd never really felt at home in either of the places that she had called home. Not up there in the windblown desolation of Level Land, and not back there on the outskirts of Comfort, on a failing family farm haunted with too much history. But here, rambling around the People's Republic of Austin for the very first time, somehow Opal already knew instinctively that she belonged here, in this otherworldly little Texas town adorned in a Violet Crown, kicking around a carefree cathedral of sound where music and weirdness abounded. She was in Austin. At long last, she was in Austin. And even though it was her first time here, she still felt like she was coming home.

As she glanced up at the darkened sky overhead, she found herself hoping that her friends in the Clothesline Crew would feel the same way. She closed her eyes and tried to picture all of them soaring over Austin together for the very first time, a winged band of orphaned and outcast melomaniacs seeking sanctuary in a tiny Texas town that also happened to be the Live Music Capital of the World....

12

THE GROOVER'S PARADISE

When Lavaca and Brazos and the rest of the Clothesline Crew reached the edge of the city, they stopped to rest on a tall metal tower with a ring of six blindingly bright arc lamps at the top. It was a giant old-timey streetlight called a moon tower that could light up a whole neighborhood as bright as the light of a full moon. There were a whole mess of moon towers spread all over Austin to help folks find their way at night.

The moon towers of Austin, Texas, are the only known surviving moon towers in the world. Each one is about 165 feet tall with a ring of six carbon arc lamps at the top that can illuminate a 1,500-foot radius. The city of Austin purchased thirty-one used moon towers from the city of Detroit in 1894, who had bought them new from the manufacturer, the Fort Wayne Electric Company of Indiana. Today, thirteen of these towers are still standing, and they still help light up the streets of Austin each night.

As the bats were all hanging there from the ladderlike rungs of the moon tower, about three-quarters of the way up, admiring the incredible panoramic view of the capital city, their extrasensitive ears began to prick up and swivel around like little radar dishes, as they each detected a faint and familiar sound drifting up to them on the warm evening wind. The sound of music! Many different overlapping melodies of music, with many different rhythms, resonating and harmonizing on a whole mess of different frequencies, forming this weird sort of polyphonic symphony of supersweet sounds that drifted through the streets of the city and echoed off its buildings and ricocheted around until it reached the recesses of the Clothesline Crew's tiny little ears, lighting up the switchboards of their tiny little melomaniac brains brighter than a Fourth of July fireworks show.

The bats all suddenly felt hypnotized. In unison, they dropped away from the moon tower and took flight again, splitting up into their usual pairs. Each pair soared off in a different direction, following the sound of a different melody to its source somewhere out there in the city.

Meanwhile, Trinity and Colorado were flying in the opposite direction, away from the city. They kept on flying until they finally rejoined the rest of their colony, which was holed up in a big old abandoned barn near the highway, about ten miles outside the city limits. The barn's weather-beaten walls were all warping inward, and half its roof had already collapsed. The bats were all huddled together under the other half, hanging from old rafters and roof beams and railings. The barn's rotting frame was creaking and bending under all the weight, and the whole place sounded like it might collapse at any moment.

Trinity and Colorado exchanged worried looks. They were running out of time to find a new home. There were thousands and thousands of expectant bat mothers in the colony who were going to start giving birth to their pups any day now. The Clothesline Crew needed to find the colony a new home before that happened, to keep all those mamas and their newborn bat babies safe from the elements and predators and all the other cruel uncertainties of life.

Trinity and Colorado gathered the colony elders together and quickly told them the plan. The rest of the colony would stay put and continue to hole up in the abandoned barn a little while longer, and the

Clothesline Crew would continue to search the city for a new home.

"A little while longer?" one of the elders repeated. "How much longer is that going to be?"

"And what if you don't find us a new home?" another elder asked. "What are we supposed to do then?"

Trinity and Colorado looked at each other and then shrugged in unison.

"I don't know," Colorado replied.

Then Trinity added, "I guess we'll cross that bridge when we come to it."

And with that, they both bid everyone farewell and streaked off into the night, flying toward the glittering Austin skyline in the distance.

Rainey and Red were both flapping their wings as fast as they could, weaving their way through the streets and alleyways of downtown Austin like a pair of tiny fighter jets, using their built-in rock-and-roll radar to zero in on the source of the incredible song they were hearing in the distance—a scorching combination of psychedelic rock and hillbilly blues unlike anything they'd ever heard before. They followed it to a giant concert hall with the words CITY COLISEUM written across it. That was where all the rocking out was coming from. The big marquee out front said that a band called ZZ Top was performing that night. Circling around, Rainey and Red spotted a big, red hot-rod automobile parked out in back of the coliseum, near its rear entrance. The car had big chrome wheels and flames and a double-Z logo painted across its sides.

The bats spotted a small open skylight on the roof of the coliseum and flew inside. They roosted up in the rafters, high above the sold-out crowd. ZZ Top was right there in front of them, down on the stage, performing to thousands of adoring fans. It was a three-man group, and the two men out in front, the guitarist and the bassist, both had really long beards. Two of the longest beards the bats had ever seen on humans. The drummer had only a mustache. All three of them were singing a song about how every girl was crazy about a sharp-dressed man, and they were really tearing it up. It was some of the best-sounding rock and roll Rainey and Red had ever heard.

It made them lose control.

They couldn't resist.

The bats both took flight and began to dance in the air, directly over the band and the enormous crowd of blissful fans, who were also singing and dancing along. Rainey and Red both fed off all that energy and then began to add their own energy to it. As they both circled over the crowd, humming and purring along with the music, the subsonic sound waves of their mojo drifted out across the entire coliseum and down into the ears and souls of all the folks out in the audience and the three musicians up onstage. The effect was instantaneous. Like an unexpected earful of auditory adrenaline. All that bat musical mojo inspired the band to rock even harder, and it made the audience roll even harder, too.

This, in turn, made Rainey and Red sing and dance harder still, causing them both to put out even more mojo, creating a feedback loop that quickly spiraled out of control, resulting in one of the greatest rock and roll shows in history. Rainey and Red thought they'd died and gone to music heaven. After the show was over, they declared that ZZ Top was their new favorite band. They used their claws to comb out the fur on their little bat chins, in an attempt to make it look as though they both had long beards like their new musical idols. Then they spotted the band leaving in their fancy red hot rod and decided to follow them. The bats wound up crashing their big after-party on the roof of a

high-rise downtown hotel. None of the boys in ZZ Top seemed to mind.

Rainey and Red were having such a good time they forgot they were supposed to be out searching for a new home. They spent the whole night rocking out with rock stars instead.

Pearl and Sabine soared over the city, following the sound of rhythm and blues music. It led them to a little place called Antone's, where a band known as the Fabulous Thunderbirds was on the stage, singing and playing their hearts out. All the people in the audience were grooving along with them as they performed a song called "Tuff Enuff." The lyrics were about some guy telling his lady how tough he was— tough enough to handle anything fate threw at him.

Pearl and Sabine both felt electrified by the words and the pulsing rhythm of the music. Like the rest of the Clothesline Crew, they'd both been feeling stressed and depressed these past few days, what with all their weary wandering through the wilderness in the wake of losing their home. But

now, hearing that Fabulous Thunderbirds song, the bats both suddenly felt like they were tough enough to handle anything fate threw at them, too. In fact, they suddenly didn't even feel like they were bats anymore. They felt like the powerful mojo of the music had just transformed both of them into fabulous thunderbirds.

Pearl and Sabine couldn't help themselves. They both took flight and began to dance in the air, circling over the stage and the crowd, basking in the best rhythm and blues music they'd ever heard!

They both began to purr and hum and emanate waves of subsonic mojo that permeated through the whole place and all the people in it. All that mojo made the Fabulous Thunderbirds play and sing better than they ever had before, and that was really saying something.

Pearl and Sabine didn't think anything would ever be able to top the show they'd just seen. But they were both in for a shock, because the show wasn't over yet. The Thunderbirds were just the opening act that night! Now the great B.B. King was taking the stage, carrying his beloved guitar Lucille! The bats were just a few feet away, directly above him, hanging from the rafters with their little jaws hanging open as he launched into the song "Night Life."

And after B.B. King tore up the stage and brought down the house, can you imagine who took the stage last, to close out the show? None other than the legendary Muddy Waters himself! And he opened with his classic rendition of a song that both bats adored: "Got My Mojo Working."

Watching Muddy Waters perform "Got My

Mojo Working" right in front of them sent Pearl and Sabine into a kind of blissed-out mojo overdrive! Neither one of them could believe their eyes! Or their ears! They were in melomaniac heaven.

From that moment on, they were both powerless to resist. They felt compelled to stay and dance and sing the rest of the night away. So they did. And somehow it slipped their minds that they were supposed to be out searching for a new home.

When they finally did remember, it still didn't matter, because they couldn't bring themselves to leave Antone's as long as the music lasted, and it lasted all night long. And afterward they didn't feel an ounce of remorse, because they both knew they'd just witnessed one the greatest shows in history, and neither one of them would have missed it for the whole wide world.

In fact, neither of them could wait to come back the following night.

When Trinity and Colorado finally reached downtown Austin, they didn't see any sign of the rest of the Clothesline Crew, so they just started to search the city on their own. They were flying over the east side of town when they spotted a cluster of old abandoned factory buildings that looked as if they might serve as a good roost.

Unfortunately, after they got their hopes up, they discovered a sign posted out front that said all those empty buildings were scheduled for demolition in a few days.

The two bats were just about to fly a little farther south to continue their search when they heard something so distracting it nearly made them collide with each other in midair. It was the sweet, intoxicating sound of country music! And not just any old country music. This was one of the most beautiful country songs the bats had ever heard. And the voice of the man singing it sounded very familiar....

Trinity and Colorado followed the sound of that voice all the way to its source, a little honky-tonk near the southern edge of town called the Broken Spoke. There was a wagon wheel with a busted spoke sitting right out in front of the place.

According to my mama, a honky-tonk was "a seedy nightclub frequented by folks who make bad life choices, where they play a lot of maudlin country music about folks who frequent seedy nightclubs and make bad life choices." People also refer to the kind of music they play in those places as honky-tonk. So I guess you know you're in a honky-tonk if you walk in and hear them playing honky-tonk.

Also, it just occurred to me that *honky-tonk* is spelled an awful lot like *Donkey Kong*. You could slap a few homemade stickers on any *Donkey Kong* machine and make folks think it was a game called *Honky-Tonk*. It would be even funnier if you did it to a *Donkey Kong* game that was in a honky-tonk! But I am not endorsing or promoting such behavior.

Trinity and Colorado snuck inside through one of the many holes in the roof so they could hear better. They perched out of sight, up in the rafters, carefully positioning themselves to get a good view of the stage. And that was when they saw him. Their country music idol, the great Willie Nelson, was standing right down there on the tiny stage, strumming on Trigger, his old beat-up acoustic guitar. Willie had a beard and long hair that he wore braided into two ponytails. He was singing and playing a song called "Texas on a Saturday Night," which was one of Trinity and Colorado's favorites. They'd seen

Willie perform it on *Austin City Limits* once, and it had filled both of their furry little hearts with joy. But it was nothing compared with the experience of seeing Willie perform it live and in person.

All the folks in the audience were dancing and singing and having a grand old time, and Trinity and Colorado couldn't resist. They had to join in, too. And the two of them filled the Broken Spoke up with so much mojo that it inspired Willie to keep on playing and the crowd to keep on dancing all night long. Trinity and Colorado had so much fun they totally lost track of time and—brace yourself for a shock—they completely forgot they were supposed to be out searching the city for a new home.

Cesar and Jacinto circled the Texas state capitol building, then flew due east, following the sweet sound of Tejano music. The melody led them across the interstate to a little dance hall on the east side of town, where a young woman named Selena was singing "Como la Flor," the most beautiful Tejano song the bats had ever heard.

Cesar and Jacinto flew in through an open window and hid up in the rafters above the stage. It wasn't long before they both fell under Selena's spell and began to sing along, filling the club up with enough mojo and making everyone enjoy the music and the performance even more, including Selena herself. She sang even louder and danced and spun even faster and put out even more mojo of her own. It was an incredible show, and the bats completely lost track of time. They forgot they were supposed to be out scouring the city, looking for a new home. And even once they remembered, they still couldn't bring themselves to leave.

Name: Selena
Full Name: Selena Quintanilla Pérez
Birthplace: Lake Jackson, Texas
Favorite Songs: Como La Flor, Dreaming of You, Baila Esta Cumbia

I read that when she was first starting out, Selena would have a hard time getting booked at a lot of the clubs around Texas because Tejano music was dominated by men at the time, and a lot of places didn't want a woman up on their stage. But Selena never let that get to her and she never gave up, and when she started making records, she became a huge superstar all around the world. She died too young, like Buddy, but just like him, she's gonna live forever, because that's how long people are gonna be enjoying her music. Forever.

Koenig and Lamar flew along the river that wound its way through the center of the city, following the distant sound of scratching vinyl and a thumping bass line. It led them to a little music venue called Liberty Lunch, where the legendary rap group Run-DMC was performing their first-ever show in Austin. The bats couldn't believe their timing! They listened to the packed-in crowd rap along to a song called "It's Like That." Koenig and Lamar had never heard anything quite like it. They just couldn't help themselves. They both took flight over the crowd and started dancing and rapping along, too, supercharging the show with their musical mojo. The whole club began to vibrate with shared energy, and Koenig and Lamar completely lost track of time. They forgot they were supposed to be looking for a new home.

Lavaca and Brazos still refused to partner up, so they were both flying solo that night, each one soaring over the city in solitude seeking sanctuary. That is, until they both heard the same beautiful melody at the same beautiful moment, floating up to them from somewhere down in the city below. Both of them began to zero in on the melody and follow it to its source—a big concert hall downtown called Palmer Auditorium, where a famous local guitarist named Eric Johnson was performing an instrumental he'd written called "Cliffs of Dover." An instrumental is a song without any lyrics or singing. Just music. And this was some of the most beautiful music Lavaca or Brazos had ever heard, and it made them both take flight and begin to dance above the city skyline. They completely forget about all their troubles. For a little while, they even seemed to forget their long-standing feud, because they began to spiral around each other up there in the sky, both so lost in the music neither of them realized they were, at long last, finally dancing together.

When the song ended, Lavaca and Brazos snapped out of their mojo trance, suddenly embarrassed, and flew off in opposite directions, each following the distant sound of a different song being played in a different corner of the weird, magical musical smorgasbord of a town spread out before them.

Like all the other melomaniac bats in the Clothesline Crew, they were powerless to resist Austin's sweet auditory charms. They both spent the rest of the night dancing and grooving and making mountains of music mojo that they broadcast out into the night. But in the process, they completely lost track of time and forgot they were supposed to be out searching for a new home.

They just couldn't help themselves. The music made them lose control.

13

MUSTA NOTTA GOTTA LOTTA SLEEP LAST NIGHT

Uncle Roscoe knew his way around town pretty well, because he'd spent a few weeks visiting Austin the summer after he finished high school, back when he was still planning to attend UT. Opal took the street map out of the glove box to help him navigate, but he didn't need it. He rambled through the darkened maze of city streets until they arrived at a little place on South Congress Avenue called the Austin Motel. He parked the Red Rambler right next to its glowing neon sign, which shined down on them like a lighthouse beacon.

Opal waited in the car while Uncle Roscoe went inside to rent them a room. After she was sitting

there for a few seconds, she noticed the sound of music being played in the distance. She craned her head out the window to try to locate its source. It appeared to be coming from an establishment down the street called the Continental Club. It had a big neon sign out front, too. Someone in there was playing a song that Opal recognized called "Me and

Billy the Kid" by Joe Ely. She used to hear it all the time on the radio when she lived up in Lubbock, because Joe Ely use to live up there, too, before he relocated to Austin.

When Uncle Roscoe emerged from the motel's office a few minutes later, Opal jumped out of the Rambler and ran over to him.

"Do you hear that, Uncle Roscoe?" she asked excitedly. "I think Joe Ely is playing down the street!"

He cocked an ear in that direction and a smile appeared on his face.

"I think you're right!" he replied, nodding toward the Continental Club. "You want to wander that way, so we can hear him a little better?"

Opal's eyes went wide in surprise.

"Can we?" she whispered.

"Sure," he said, whispering back. "You're too young to get inside, but you can usually hear the band pretty good if you stand by the back door. I did that a time or two when I didn't have enough dough for the door charge. Follow me and I'll show you."

She took his hand, and they both made sure to look both ways before crossing the street. Once they reached the Continental Club, Uncle Roscoe led Opal around to the building's rear entrance. The back door was propped open, so they could hear the music perfectly, even though they couldn't see the band. There was a big, muscular bald man in a denim jacket standing in the open doorway, like a guard. He didn't look very friendly to Opal, but he didn't ask them to leave. So she and Uncle Roscoe just stood there for a while, listening and enjoying the music.

When the band launched into the beginning of its next song, "Musta Notta Gotta Lotta," it had such a great beat that Opal couldn't help herself. She started dancing along to it. Uncle Roscoe watched her for a few seconds, and then he started to dance with her. He twirled her around in circles a few times, then hunched down so Opal could spin him around a few times, too.

For some reason, watching the two of them get down put a big old grin on the big bald guy's face. When the song ended, he waved them over.

"You cats really know how to cut a rug," he said. He took a quick look around before lowering his voice to a whisper. "If you want, you can stand just inside the back door for a while, so you can see the band from behind the stage."

"Wow, really?" Opal whispered back. "Thank you!"

"No problem," he said. "But if anyone asks, you snuck past me. Deal?"

Opal and Uncle Roscoe both nodded.

"Deal," they replied in unison.

He stepped aside and they stepped inside. They stood just a few feet from the back door, with their backs against the wall. From there, Opal was able to see most of the stage and part of the audience. And she could hear everything!

Opal had been listening to music her whole life, but this was the first time she had ever seen or heard it performed in person. Unless you counted her church choir or junior high school marching band, which Opal most definitely did not.

Seeing one of your favorite songs performed live is totally different from listening to it on the radio. When Opal was standing right there, just a few feet away from the musicians, she could feel the energy coming off them and their instruments up there on the stage. At the same time, she could also feel the energy coming from all the other people around her in the audience, all singing and grooving and moving together as if their hearts and minds were connected.

That was when Opal realized that, under the right circumstances, humans could make mojo, too. And when they did, it was contagious.

Everyone there at the Continental Club that night, including Opal, could feel all that shared mojo filling up the room and filling up their hearts, until it finally transported everyone who was playing and singing and everyone who was listening and dancing to a whole other world of sound and energy and joy that would be impossible to describe with words, so I ain't even gonna try.

Suffice it to say, Opal and Uncle Roscoe both completely lost track of time. They forgot they had to get up early in the morning to start searching for a new home. For the time being, they forgot about all their troubles, and the bats' troubles, too. They decided to let tomorrow sort itself out and gave themselves over to the music.

The next morning at dawn, when all the members of the Clothesline Crew met back up at the moon tower, they were more than a little disheartened to learn that none of them had managed to find a new home for the colony, even though they'd all been out searching all night long. But when Lavaca and Brazos asked everyone exactly *where* they'd searched, it quickly became evident none of them had done a lick of searching at all. Instead, the whole lot of them had wasted the entire night away listening and grooving to live music! And it wasn't like Lavaca and Brazos could be upset with the others, since they were both guilty of doing the same thing.

Brazos decided that the complete and total lapse of willpower the Clothesline Crew had exhibited wasn't really their fault. They were melomaniacs, after all. And there was just too much great music being played in this city every night. There was no way they would ever be able to ignore it. Or resist following it. But one thing was clear. All twelve of the bats in the Clothesline Crew had fallen head over heels in love with Austin, and now they were all even more desperate to find a new home than before.

After a heated discussion, Lavaca finally came up with an incredibly simple solution to their dilemma. She suggested they all change up their sleeping schedule. From now on, they would sleep at night and search for a home during the day, when there

wouldn't be as many ridiculously talented musicians around to distract them.

The rest of the Clothesline Crew agreed that this was an excellent plan. But none of them was ready to put it into action immediately. They were all exhausted from a long night of grooving and spreading their mojo all over town. They needed some sleep *now*, before they switched to the day shift, so they decided to stay put and take a nice long nap right there on the moon tower. Once everyone was rested up, they could continue their search. And this time, they promised one another not to let themselves get distracted by the sights and sounds of the city.

It wasn't a promise they were able to keep.

14

THIS MUST BE THE PLACE

That same morning, Uncle Roscoe took Opal out to breakfast at a place called Magnolia Cafe. It was filled with some of the weirdest and most interesting-looking people she'd ever seen. Their waitress was a really cool-looking tattooed lady in cut-off jeans and a cowboy hat who also wore a nose ring and big red boots. Opal immediately decided that she wanted to dress the same way when she grew up. (Except maybe for the nose ring. She was afraid that would hurt.)

After they ordered food, Uncle Roscoe bought a newspaper and looked through the classified ads for a job and a house they could rent. He circled the best prospects with a red pen while Opal devoured a giant stack of blueberry pancakes. He ate a plate of something called migas, along with four or five breakfast tacos. Uncle Roscoe told her that it was tradition to eat Mexican food for your very first breakfast in Austin, and for every breakfast after that, too. But that seemed too weird for Opal, and besides, she wanted pancakes.

After breakfast, they rambled up Congress Avenue to the office of the local newspaper, which was called the *Austin American-Statesman*. It was located right on the shore of Town Lake. Uncle Roscoe had rambled down there to apply for a job opening he'd just read about in the *Statesman* classifieds earlier that morning. The newspaper wanted to hire a computer expert to help its reporters transition from writing their articles on typewriters to using computer word processors instead. The ad said it was just a two-month-long temp job, but that it could lead to something permanent.

Uncle Roscoe was nervous and excited, because he thought he had a decent shot at getting the gig, if he didn't blow the interview. Before he went inside, he put on a fancy button-up shirt and a clip-on necktie out in the parking lot. Then he handed Opal his hat while he checked his hair in the driver's-side mirror.

"Do you mind waiting for me out here in the Red Rambler?" he asked. "This shouldn't take too long. I left the keys in the ignition so you can listen to the radio. But no drag racing!"

"You know I don't know how to drive, silly," Opal replied, helping her uncle straighten his tie. Then she rested her hands on his shoulders and looked him in the eyes. "Good luck in there. Not that you'll need it. You know more about computers than anyone I've ever met, and you're great at teaching people to use them. So just be yourself."

He nodded and gave her a smile.

"Thanks, Opal," he said. Then he took a deep breath and strode off toward the giant newspaper building's imposing front entrance, adding, "Here goes nothing!"

After she watched him disappear inside, Opal switched on the radio. A song she'd always loved happened to be on, called "This Must Be the Place

(Naive Melody)" by Talking Heads. As she listened to its sweet melody, she rolled down her window and leaned out to get a better look at her surroundings. It was still early in the day, so it wasn't hot out yet. And there was a nice breeze blowing in over the water. Opal turned her head to feel it blowing against her cheek, and that was when she spotted it, towering directly overhead....

The Congress Avenue Bridge was refurbished in the early 1980s. Long narrow gaps were built into the structure to allow the concrete to expand and retract in the cold without cracking. The bridge stretched across a dammed-up section of the Colorado River that the locals called Town Lake, even though it technically wasn't a river or a lake. It was a reservoir.

It was a bridge! A big old beautiful bridge on Congress Avenue that stretched all the way across Town Lake, connecting the south side of the city to the north side.

Opal jumped out of the Rambler and sprinted across the parking lot to get a closer look, and that was when she discovered something wonderful.

On the underside of the massive bridge, she spotted a series of long narrow gaps built into the concrete. They were spaced every few feet, and each gap was just over an inch wide—just wide enough for a bat to crawl up inside, but too narrow for any mean old hawks or owls or other predators to follow them. Opal's heart began to race as she realized what she was looking at. The entire underside of the Congress Avenue Bridge was like a giant high-rise apartment building made especially for her little free-tailed bat friends! It looked like there were half a dozen of those long narrow gaps, and they ran the entire length of the bridge. Opal could already tell there would be more than enough room for the entire colony to fit in there. With plenty of space left over for it to grow.

It was perfect.

As she was standing there, gazing up at the bridge in awe, she felt a small twinge of pain as something bit into her right forearm. She looked down to see a mosquito there and slapped it away. As she did, she felt another mosquito bite her on the leg, and then another one got her on the back of the neck. As she brushed them away with her hands and took a quick look at her surroundings, she spotted several little black clouds of mosquitoes buzzing and swarming all around the bridge. Which made perfect sense, because it stretched over Town Lake, and mosquitoes love to hang out near pools of standing water because that's where the little bloodsuckers lay their eggs. That was why she was getting eaten alive right now! There were a bunch of small pools of standing water along the shores of Town Lake. She was standing in the middle of a giant mosquito breeding ground—

Which meant it would also be a perfect bat feeding ground!

Opal let out a triumphant holler as she ran back to the Red Rambler and scrambled inside and slammed the door shut. She rolled up the windows as quickly as she could, then began swatting at all the mosquitoes that had managed to get inside with her, all while grinning from ear to ear. She had never been so happy about getting covered in mosquito bites in her entire life. She couldn't believe her luck. Not only had she found a place big enough for over a million bats to live, but it was also located right next to a food source abundant enough to feed all of them!

It was as if the lyrics of the song on the radio were speaking directly to her. *I guess that this must be the place....*

Just then, Opal spotted Uncle Roscoe slowly strutting back over to the Rambler with a big smile on his face. Opal jumped out and ran across the parking lot to meet him.

"Great news, kiddo!" he shouted, giving her double high fives. "I got the job! They asked me to start in a few days!"

"Congratulations, Uncle Roscoe!" she replied, throwing her arms around him. "That *is* great news!" She turned and pointed toward the bridge. "I've got some pretty great news, too. Look what I just found!"

He looked up at the bridge, then back at Opal, furrowing his brow in confusion. "What?" he replied. "You mean the bridge?"

She nodded.

"But that isn't just any bridge," Opal replied, spreading both of her arms out wide, as if she were presenting the grand prize on a game show. "That is the big old beautiful bridge where all our furry little flying friends are going to live from now on. It's their new home!"

His eyes widened in surprise. But before he could respond, she grabbed her uncle's hand and began to run back toward the car, pulling him along with her.

"Come on!" she shouted. "We need to find the Clothesline Crew right away so they can check it out!"

They spent the next few hours rambling around downtown in circles, searching for the Clothesline Crew. But there was no sign of them.

"Maybe they already found another spot to roost?" Uncle Roscoe suggested. "Or maybe they gave up and flew off to rejoin the rest of their colony?"

Opal shook her head. When she closed her eyes and concentrated, she sensed that the bats were somewhere close by, but she couldn't seem to get a fix on their exact location. Then, just as Opal was beginning to get really worried, she happened to glance up and spotted all twelve of the bats in the Clothesline Crew, hanging from the top rungs of a moon tower a few blocks from their motel.

"There they are!" she cried, pointing them out to her uncle. "It looks like the poor little things had a long night."

"Yeah," he replied, grinning up at them. "And now it looks like they're having themselves a little self-pity party at the moon tower. Let's go tell them the good news!"

They rambled over and parked the Red Rambler near the base of the moon tower. Uncle Roscoe had to honk his horn a few times to wake the bats up. When they finally opened their eyes and spotted Opal waving up at them excitedly, the entire Clothesline Crew flew down to hear what she had to say.

"I think we've found the perfect new home for you and your entire bat family!" she proclaimed as they hovered around her. "There's a giant bridge just over there on Congress Avenue, with these long gaps underneath that are just big enough for y'all to fit inside. There should be enough room for your entire family!"

She climbed back into the Rambler and her uncle joined her. Then Opal waved at the bats, motioning for them to follow.

"Come on!" she hollered up at them. "We'll show you!"

Uncle Roscoe rambled the Rambler back over to the bridge with the Clothesline Crew trailing close behind. They parked in the *Statesman*'s lot again, and Opal and her uncle watched through the windshield as the Clothesline Crew laid eyes on the big old beautiful bridge for the first time. All twelve of them began to chitter and squeak excitedly as they circled around it, scoping the place out. One by one, they disappeared into the narrow gaps in the concrete on its underside, then they emerged as a group a few minutes later, all of them squeaking excitedly and grinning from ear to ear.

"They love it!" Opal told Uncle Roscoe. "They think it's perfect! And big enough for everyone! They're going to tell the rest of the colony and guide them back here."

The bats suddenly flew off in unison, headed toward the city outskirts. Opal watched them go.

Once they were out of sight, she closed her eyes and focused her thoughts on her furry flying friends, following their progress with her mind's eye.

When the Clothesline Crew reached the rest of the colony, they gathered everyone together to share the good news with them. Then, after some cajoling, they persuaded everyone to follow them back into town to see their new home under the big old beautiful bridge for themselves.

When they reached it, the bridge was silhouetted perfectly against the setting sun. Its curved underside formed a half circle with the water's flat surface, which made it resemble the half-circle-shaped mouth of the big old beautiful cave. It made the bats feel like they were coming home. The elder bats couldn't believe their good fortune! Everything the Clothesline Crew had told them was true. It was like the city had constructed a giant bat hotel for them under the bridge. Those narrow gaps in the concrete made a perfect bat roost. There was more

than enough room for all of them to fit safely inside. And the colony would have plenty of room to grow.

Best of all, there were billions of delicious mosquitoes everywhere they looked. It was like having an all-you-can-eat bug buffet right next to their brand-new high-rise bat hotel.

It really did seem like they'd discovered the perfect place for their new home. That is, until the rest of the city found out they were there.

15

PANIC ON THE STREETS OF AUSTIN

You can probably imagine how the people of Austin reacted that evening when they wandered outside to admire another gorgeous Violet Crown sunset and suddenly saw a million bats flying out from under the Congress Avenue Bridge for the first time, darkening the sky overhead. Most of these folks had only ever seen bats in horror movies, so they assumed that *all* bats were rabid vampires who wanted nothing more than to bite their necks and suck their blood. So when the people of Austin saw a giant horde of them fill the sky over their fair city, a good number of them freaked out. Folks were running around their neighborhoods whooping and hollering like their

hair was on fire. More than one person crashed their car into a tree or a telephone pole because their eyes were glued to the sky and not the road.

Opal and Uncle Roscoe didn't realize just how bad a first impression the bats had made on the people of Austin until the following morning, when they were having breakfast tacos at an incredibly inexpensive and thus extremely busy little place called Tamale House #3. They were sitting outside

EXCLUSIVE!
MUCKERNO LIMESTONE
EXPANSION PLANS FOR
NEXT YEAR: PAGE 5.

INTERVIEW
ANN RICHARDS
SPEAKS OUT

BEVO

HELPS LONGHORN
WIN AGAINST O.U.

WEATHER
HIGH: 108F
SUNNY
CHANCE OF
RAIN: 0%

Austin American-Statesman

35 CENTS   PUBLISHED SINCE 1871

Mexican free-tailed bats flit eerily under a cloak of darkness as they emerge from the Congress Avenue Bridge.

BAT COLONIES SINK TEETH INTO CITY!

at a little table near the front entrance when Uncle Roscoe glanced at the front page of a newspaper someone else had left behind. It was a copy of that morning's *Austin American-Statesman*. The headline covered half of the front page:

BAT COLONIES SINK TEETH INTO CITY!

The article was written by some smug-looking reporter named Wiley Woodbern. This Woodbern fella obviously wasn't too happy about a million bats taking up residence under the bridge that stood right next to his workplace, because he'd stayed up all night writing a nasty, misinformed screed about it for the front page of the local newspaper. The same newspaper Uncle Roscoe had to start working at in a few days. He couldn't believe it.

After the first few paragraphs, Uncle Roscoe was too upset to read any further, so he asked Opal if she would read the rest of it to him. She reluctantly obliged. There was a long line of people who were waiting to get their food standing nearby, and Opal knew a bunch of them were probably eavesdropping on their conversation. But she went ahead and read the rest of the article aloud anyway.

Each sentence of it seemed to make her angrier than the previous one, and her voice got louder and more disbelieving the further she read. The entire article was filled with exaggerations and inaccuracies that made it sound like the newly arrived bats were a serious threat to the community. Woodbern implied that the entire colony was probably infected with rabies, and he also cited an "unverified report" that several of these "obviously rabid" bats had already attacked unwitting pedestrians crossing the bridge, without any provocation whatsoever.

"Lies!" Opal shouted at the front page. "None of this garbage is true! None of those bats have rabies! And they didn't attack anyone last night, either, except for a few billion bugs!" She turned to her uncle. "Why would the newspaper publish an article that's just trying to scare everyone?"

"Because scared people buy newspapers," he replied. "That's why they always put the scariest thing they can find at the top of the front page each day, in big bold letters. If it's scary enough, then folks feel like they have to buy it and read the article to find out exactly what they're supposed to be scared of and how scared of it they're supposed to be. It's a racket, kiddo."

She continued reading, and he continued to listen. Near the end of the article, when Woodbern referred to the newly arrived colony of bats under the bridge as the "Congress Avenue Cauldron," for some reason it made Uncle Roscoe hopping mad. He really went off about it.

"*Cauldron* is not an acceptable collective noun for a bunch of bats!" he declared, a little too loudly. "It's basically a slur! And it's used only by callous-hearted cretins to reinforce the existing negative stereotypes about bats fostered by mainstream horror films! The only reason anyone would refer to them as a 'cauldron' instead of a 'colony' is to frighten people, because everyone associates cauldrons with witches and potions and cannibals and such." He shook his head. "The bats are here less than twenty-four hours, and the local media is already trying to stigmatize them."

He took the newspaper from her and held it up.

"Well, I'll tell you what—when I start working at this paper, I'm gonna introduce myself to this Wiley Woodbern fella and help him straighten out a few of his facts."

He dropped the newspaper in a trash can. Opal immediately took it back out. Then she tore off part of the front page containing the bat article and began taping it into her scratchbook with long strips of cellophane tape.

"You're saving that?" Uncle Roscoe asked in disbelief. "Why?"

"As a reminder," she said angrily. "That Austin is just like everywhere else."

"Hey now," he said, softening his tone. "Don't say that. This is just a little bad press in the local paper. That's all. Most people read the *Austin Chronicle* anyway because it's free, and they don't print nearly as many outright lies on their front page. So cheer up! This isn't the end of the world."

Her expression brightened a little.

"Are you sure about that?"

"Positive," he replied. "Trust me. The situation could be so much worse...."

He was right. The situation could and did get so much worse. And it happened quite quickly.

That evening, Opal and Uncle Roscoe were watching TV in their room at the Austin Motel when a story about the bats came on the local news. It was even worse than the *Statesman* article. It began with a news reporter standing on the Congress Avenue Bridge at sunset, as the bats streamed out from under it and up into the sky behind him. He repeated the nonsense claims from the paper about the bats being infected with rabies and attacking people. But they never named or showed any of the people who claimed to have been attacked. Instead, they cut to an interview with an ill-tempered Austin city councilman named Lyle Muckerno, who said he was going to make it his personal mission to eradicate the "flying rodents" who had "infested" the bridge, using every means at the city's disposal.

He said the local humane society had a team of dogcatchers who were now going to be reassigned as full-time bat catchers, tasked with hunting them down.

"If necessary, our pest-control department can use blowtorches and flamethrowers to force all those vile little creatures out of those cracks under the bridge," Councilman Muckerno said, smiling into the television cameras. "Then we can cover all those cracks with wire screens to prevent them from ever moving back in. I plan to propose this course of action at the next city council meeting."

Uncle Roscoe shut off the TV, and then he and Opal stared at each other for a moment in shock.

"Councilman Muckerno?" Opal repeated. "As in Muckerno Limestone?"

Uncle Roscoe nodded. "His family owns that limestone company," he said. "And a lot of other companies, too. That's why he weaseled his way onto the city council—so he could lobby for all of his family's environmentally destructive business interests."

Opal was flabbergasted at the injustice of it. Muckerno's company had driven the bats out of their previous home with bulldozers and dynamite, and now he was trying to run them out of their new home, too, with blowtorches and flamethrowers.

"Why do you think he hates bats so much?" Opal asked.

"I couldn't say," Uncle Roscoe said. "The Muckernos seem to hate everyone and everything. I reckon some families just have a mile-wide mean streak running through them, the same way we have a mile-wide weird streak running through ours."

"I'll take a weird streak over a mean streak any day," Opal said.

"Amen to that!" he replied. "Spoken like a true Flats!"

Opal stood up, walked over to the door of their room, and threw it open.

"Come on," she said, glancing back at her uncle expectantly. "Let's go."

"Go where?" he asked.

"To find the Clothesline Crew!" she replied. "We need to tell them the bad news. And come up with a plan to fight back."

Opal asked her uncle to ramble them back over to the moon tower. Once they reached it, she placed her right hand on the tower and closed her eyes, then tried to use her newfound psychic powers to summon the Clothesline Crew. She thought holding on to the moon tower while she did it might amplify her ability, sort of like a big antenna. It seemed to work, because a few minutes later the different members of the Clothesline Crew began to arrive one after the other, until all twelve of them were hanging in front of her, suspended from the lowest rungs of the moon tower.

Opal told the Clothesline Crew about all the negative media coverage they'd received in the paper and on TV, and about Councilman Muckerno's plans to drive them out of their new home under the bridge with blowtorches and flamethrowers, and then cover up the gaps on its underside with wire screens to keep them out.

The Clothesline Crew was mortified. None of them knew what to do. They were the ones who had persuaded the rest of their colony to risk everything and move here. And now their worst fear already seemed to be coming true. Their whole colony was about to become homeless again, and the bats didn't have anywhere else to go. And even if they did, the yearly litter of pups had already started to arrive, and the baby bat pups were still too young to fly on their own. The colony couldn't leave now.

Besides that, they didn't *want* to leave! They loved their new home under the big old beautiful bridge, and they weren't hurting anyone by being there. It was the opposite. They were trying to help make the city a better place. The Clothesline Crew didn't understand why people couldn't just leave their colony alone.

Opal didn't know what to tell them. She didn't understand it, either.

"I'm starting to feel mighty guilty about that stupid speech I gave them out at the city limit sign," Uncle Roscoe said, hanging his head. "I promised them they would all fit right in here. What was I thinking?"

"But you were right, Uncle Roscoe!" she replied. "They *do* fit right in! Austin prides itself on being the weirdest town in Texas, right? Well, what could be weirder than a million bug-eating bats living under a bridge downtown? They'd make the perfect mascots for this city! The bats belong beneath the bridge! The people of Austin just don't realize it yet. So we have to help them...."

"And how do we do that?" he asked.

Opal didn't answer right away, because her eyes had just fallen on the three brand-new stickers Uncle Roscoe had purchased and applied to the Red Rambler's rear bumper earlier that day. The first one said ONLY IN AUSTIN. The second one said ONWARD THROUGH THE FOG. And the last one had KEEP AUSTIN WEIRD printed on it in groovy tie-dye-colored letters. Opal had been seeing all three of those slogans constantly since they arrived in town, on bumper stickers and T-shirts and flyers taped up in storefront windows. But the one she saw and heard most frequently was KEEP AUSTIN WEIRD, and those were the words running through her head now, along with something she'd just said a few seconds ago... *the bats belong beneath the bridge.*

"We need a catchy slogan that will help us spread the word all over town," Opal replied, pointing at his bumper stickers. "And the perfect one just came to me...."

She took a pen out of her pocket and began using

it to write something across the knuckles of her left hand. When she was done, she made a fist and held it out so Uncle Roscoe could see what she'd drawn there—four capital letter *B*s in a row, one on the front of each knuckle.

"*The bats belong beneath the bridge!*" Opal shouted triumphantly, raising her fist to the sky.

The Clothesline Crew all began to chitter and flap their wings excitedly, as if in approval. They seemed to like it. And so did Uncle Roscoe.

"*The bats belong beneath the bridge!*" he repeated, smiling. "Wow, Opal, that is catchy!"

He took Opal's pen and used it to draw a capital letter *B* on each of the four knuckles of his right hand. Then he made a fist and showed it to Opal before raising it to the sky.

"*The bats belong beneath the bridge!*" he shouted.

"*The bats belong beneath the bridge!*" Opal echoed, raising her fist to the sky again, too.

Then they both continued to shout their new slogan over and over again, one after the other, at the top of their lungs. When they both finally ran out of breath and stopped a few seconds later, they were surprised to hear several other nearby voices shouting the slogan back at them.

"The bats belong beneath the bridge!"

She and Uncle Roscoe turned to see a blue convertible full of college kids idling on the curb behind them. They'd overheard Opal and her uncle, and now they were shouting their new slogan back at them.

"The bats belong beneath the bridge!" the kids all shouted again, waving and laughing as the convertible pulled away and drove off down the street.

Opal and her uncle both waved and shouted their new slogan back to them once more, just before the convertible rounded a corner and disappeared into the night.

Uncle Roscoe watched it go, then he put his arm around Opal and smiled.

"How about that?" he said. "The word is already spreading!"

Opal grinned and nodded. Then she turned back to look at the members of the Clothesline Crew, who were all still hanging from the rungs of the moon tower with the glittering Austin city skyline spread out behind them.

"Listen, y'all," Opal said. "Here's the plan. We need y'all to fly out across this city and try to help every person you see! You need to figure out a way to befriend all of Austin's students, politicians, and, most of all, its musicians! If you can do that, there's no way Councilman Muckerno will be able to force you out of your new home. Me and Uncle Roscoe are both gonna do everything we can to help you win everyone over. All right?"

The bats all began to chitter and squeak as they conferred among themselves. Then they nodded in unison and took flight, soaring up into the sky.

"Good luck, gang!" Opal said. "I know you can pull this off, if you use your mojo!"

16

MEETING FRIENDS AT THE FRIENDS

The following morning, Uncle Roscoe and Opal rambled up to a neighborhood bordering the Drag on the west side of the UT campus to look at a few houses for rent in that area. Uncle Roscoe said it was one of the least expensive neighborhoods to live in, because no one wanted to live near the university except students, and they usually didn't have much money, so the rent around there was usually pretty cheap. And Uncle Roscoe said there were always lots of places available during the summer, since most of the UT students had gone home for summer vacation.

He was right. They found a cozy little house

for rent just a few blocks from the Drag, which was the local nickname for Guadalupe Street, the long business-lined lane bordering the university. It was a tiny blue two-bedroom cottage with hardwood floors and push-button light switches and a tiny little backyard with a big old Texas live oak tree that made it nice and shady. It also came furnished, with lots of groovy brown, yellow, and orange furniture from the previous decade. Opal really loved the place. She thought it was cozy.

After Uncle Roscoe signed the lease and picked up the keys, they checked out of the Austin Motel and moved into their new place that same day. Unpacking didn't take them very long, because they didn't have much stuff, aside from their clothes and records, all of Uncle Roscoe's computer equipment, and the boxes containing Opal's entire collection of scratchbooks. Her new bedroom had a bookshelf built into the wall that was the perfect size to hold all of them, with room for a few more. She took it as a good sign.

When they finished unpacking, they rambled over to a brand-new grocery store called Whole

Foods that had just opened up and bought a bunch of food to fill up their new kitchen. But by the time they brought it home and put it all away, Uncle Roscoe said he didn't feel like cooking, so they decided to venture out into their new neighborhood and look for a place to have dinner. As they made their way down to the Drag, they spotted a small restaurant on the corner. It had a small outside seating area under a striped awning with the words *Les Amis* printed on it in cursive letters.

"What does *Les Amis* mean, Uncle Roscoe?" Opal asked.

"It's French," he replied. "I think it means 'The Friends.'" Then he shrugged and added, "I'm not sure, though. I took Spanish in high school."

"The Friends," Opal repeated softly. "Can we go there and try it out?"

"Sure, why not?" he said, motioning for her to lead the way. "We only live a few blocks away. If we like the food, we can eat here all the time."

They walked under the striped Les Amis awning and sat down at one of the outdoor tables adjacent to the sidewalk. It turned out to be a perfect spot for people watching, because there was a nonstop stream of them strolling by just a few feet away. It was like an endless parade of the wildest and weirdest and most welcoming-looking folks Opal had ever seen. She and Uncle Roscoe watched them with fascination for a few minutes, but they were both distracted by the big blackflies that kept buzzing around them and the mosquitoes that kept biting them.

Opal found herself wishing that some of her bat friends would show up to eat the wretched things. And then, just a few minutes later, Lavaca and Brazos did show up, both suddenly appearing out of nowhere. They flew over and hung upside down from the awning and took a long look around, scanning the area with their eyes and ears. Then they began to zip around and gobble up all the flies and mosquitoes that had been bothering and biting Opal and her uncle. It took them only a few minutes to completely clear the place out. The bugs that didn't get eaten all fled for their lives. Then Lavaca and Brazos hung upside down from the Les Amis awning to stand guard and scare off any other bugs that decided to show up.

That was when the door of the restaurant flew

open and their waitress came hurrying out. She was short with curly black hair and brown skin and a big friendly smile. She looked like she was quite a bit older than Uncle Roscoe, but that didn't seem to matter to him. He was smitten with Maria from the moment he looked up from his menu and saw her for the first time. His jaw went slack, his eyes glazed over, and his pupils practically turned into two little hearts. Opal had never seen her uncle like this before, and she found it hilarious and adorable.

"Hola, I'm Maria!" she said as she reached their table. "Sorry to keep you waiting. I'm afraid we didn't see y'all sitting out here until just now. Are you sure you don't want to sit inside? I know it's a beautiful day, but most folks have stopped eating out here, because the flies and mosquitoes have gotten so bad…."

She glanced around the outdoor seating area in bewilderment.

"Though, oddly, I don't see a single one at the moment," she continued. "No flies or mosquitoes anywhere. That's weird…."

"It's because I just asked my two bat friends over

there to get rid of them," Opal replied, pointing up at the two tiny bats hanging from the awning overhead.

When Maria glanced up and spotted them, she looked a little surprised but not the least bit frightened. Instead, she seemed genuinely delighted by them.

"Well, look at you two cute little critters!" she said, tilting her head upside down to get a better look at them. "Do they have names?"

Opal nodded. "That's Lavaca on the left and Brazos there on the right."

"Hello, Lavaca and Brazos!" Maria said, waving to them. "Thanks for eating up all those bugs! I can't tell you how much we appreciate it!"

Lavaca and Brazos both chirped and clicked a few times in reply.

"They say 'you're welcome,'" Opal translated.

Maria laughed and smiled her enormous smile at Opal. Then she smiled it at Uncle Roscoe, too. He looked like he was about to fall out of his chair.

"What about you two?" Maria asked them. "Do y'all have names?"

"Yes, we do!" Opal replied. "I'm Opal and this is my uncle, Roscoe. We just moved to town!" She jerked a thumb over her shoulder. "Our new house is just a few blocks that way."

"Oh, really?" Maria replied, jerking her own thumb in the opposite direction. "Well, my house is just a few blocks that way. We're practically neighbors." She stuck out her hand. "So welcome to the neighborhood, neighbors!"

"Thank you!" Opal replied, shaking with her.

Then Maria shook hands with Uncle Roscoe, too. But when she was done, Uncle Roscoe was so hypnotized by her beauty that he forgot to let go of her hand, until Opal kicked him in the shins a few times under the table to snap him out of it.

"Sorry!" he blurted out, releasing her hand. "I guess I spaced out there for a minute."

"That's all right," Maria replied, grinning. "I didn't mind at all."

He grinned back at her, and then the two of them just kept on grinning at each other like a couple of goofballs until Opal finally got fed up and loudly cleared her throat. Then Maria took their dinner order and disappeared back inside the restaurant. She must've shared the good news about the bug-eating bats with all the customers sitting inside, because a few seconds later, a bunch of people began to file outside, carrying their drinks and food with them as they moved to sit at one of the outdoor tables and enjoy the fresh air.

When Maria came back with their food, Opal tried to get Uncle Roscoe to start up a conversation with her, but it didn't go very well. Opal could tell that her uncle was sweet on Maria. But he was also too nervous around her to say more than a few words at a time. So Opal kept asking Maria a bunch of personal questions every time she came back to their table, to try to help her uncle out a little. That's how they learned that Maria was taking a few art classes at UT, and that she was also a single mom.

"I have a daughter named Elena who is about the same age as you," she told Opal. "I think you two might have a lot in common. I'll introduce you, if you're still here when she stops by with Mellow. She's out taking him for a walk right now."

Opal assumed that Mellow was the name of their dog, but she was mistaken.

She discovered this about fifteen minutes later, when a young girl around Opal's age walked in off the sidewalk and sat down at one of the empty tables nearby. That was when Opal noticed she was holding on to a leash, and that there appeared to be a giant armored alien rat at the other end of it.

Opal froze, resisting the urge to jump out of her chair and scream. She watched as the giant armored alien rat thing nuzzled up against the girl's right leg; then it abruptly plopped down and curled itself into a ball at her feet, like a dog. It took Opal a moment to realize that the creature was an armadillo. She'd never seen one this big before, or this ugly. It was also the first time she'd ever seen one wearing a collar or walking around on a leash. But none of the other customers were paying any attention to the creature. Opal and Uncle Roscoe were the only ones who appeared to be alarmed by its presence.

The girl pulled a large book out of her satchel and placed it on the table in front of her. It was covered in all sorts of stickers and decals for different bands, and when she opened it up, Opal saw it was a sketchbook filled with the girl's drawings. She opened it to a blank page and began to sketch something with a pencil, while the armadillo lay at her feet, flipping its enormous tail back and forth.

A few minutes later, Maria came back outside, and when she spotted the girl she hurried over to give her a hug. The two of them conferred for a moment; then the girl stood up, and Maria led her over to their table to introduce everyone.

"This is my daughter, Elena," she said. "Elena, I'd like you to meet Opal and her uncle, Roscoe. They just moved into the neighborhood."

"It's nice to meet you both," Elena said. "This here is Mellow, our nine-banded Texas armadillo. We raised him after his mama got squashed by a car when he was a baby, so he doesn't really know how to behave like an armadillo. He thinks he's some sort of weird-looking dog. You can pet him if you like. He won't mind."

Opal hesitated for a moment, then slowly reached down and ran her hand over the armadillo's scaly banded armor a few times. Mellow must've

liked it, because he started rubbing the back of his scaly little head against her ankles. This made Opal squeal, and that made everyone else laugh.

"Opal has some interesting pets, too," Maria told Elena. "Look up there."

She pointed up at Lavaca and Brazos, who were still hanging from the awning overhead.

"That's who we have to thank for getting rid of all the mosquitoes!" she added.

Like her mother, the girl looked delighted instead of scared.

"Wow!" Elena exclaimed. "You've got two pet bats?"

"Not really," Opal replied. "They're more like our friends. And there's about a million of them. We convinced their whole colony to move here with us. They're living under the Congress Avenue Bridge downtown."

Elena and Maria both smiled and nodded, as if this were the most natural thing in the world.

"Opal is really interested in drawing, too," Maria told her daughter. She pointed at Opal's sketchbook on the table. "See, she carries a sketchbook around with her all the time, just like you do."

Elena's eyes lit up when she saw it. She grabbed Opal by the forearm.

"Hey, I'll let you look through my sketchbook if you let me look through yours," she said. "What do you say?"

"Sure, okay!" Opal replied.

Opal went over and joined Elena at her table, and the two of them traded sketchbooks; then they began to page through them together, talking excitedly and complimenting each other's drawings.

Maria and Uncle Roscoe watched them for a moment, and then, to his surprise, she suddenly sat down and tried to start up a conversation with him. But he was still too nervous and tongue-tied to say more than a few words to her at a time. That was when Maria noticed the circuit board affixed to the front of his cowboy hat and complimented him on it.

"I love your hat," she said. "It makes you look like a computer cowboy."

"Thank you," he replied, blushing. "I—I'm really into computers."

That was all he could get out. Then he fell silent and started fidgeting again. She studied him for a moment, then she recited the magic words:

"You know, I've been thinking about buying a home computer," Maria said. "But I don't know much about them, so I'm not sure which kind to get."

Uncle Roscoe's eyes lit up. It was like she'd just flipped a giant switch on his back. His nervousness instantly vanished, and he began talking a mile a minute, telling her about all the different home computers that were available and what each of them could do. Maria was genuinely interested in what he was saying, and before long the two of them were talking back and forth with each other excitedly, while Opal and Elena did the same thing a few tables over.

All four of them talked up a storm, becoming fast friends in the process.

And Lavaca and Brazos remained on guard the whole time, eating up any mosquitoes that tried to bite people and any flies that tried to land on people's food. The customers ended up enjoying their dinners so much they all left huge tips for Maria and the other waitresses working there that day.

Maria was so grateful to Lavaca and Brazos for making her customers happy, she put out a plate of pineapple slices for them to eat. But they both already had bellies full of bugs, so they just nibbled at the pineapple to be polite.

During her conversation with Elena, Opal learned they had several other things in common. Elena had lost her daddy, too, to cancer, a few years earlier. After he died, she and her mama had relocated from El Paso to Austin to get a fresh start, and so far they really liked it.

Opal told Elena about moving in with Uncle

Roscoe after her mama died, and then about moving again to Austin a few days ago after losing their farm. She also told her all about bringing the bats to town with them and helping them find the bridge. Then she finished up by sharing her plan to help the bats win over the people of Austin and persuade the city council to let them stay.

Elena listened to all of this intently, then shrugged and shook her head.

"I wish you the best of luck, Opal," she said. "But you might have a harder time convincing folks to let those bats stay than you think."

"Why do you say that?" Opal asked, frowning involuntarily.

"Because of their name," Elena replied. "They're 'Mexican free-tailed bats,' right?" She smiled and exaggerated her Texas accent. "Do you think all the nice folks who live and work around that bridge want a bunch of homeless Mexicans moving into their neighborhood? Human, bat, or otherwise? I'm afraid not."

Opal furrowed her brow in confusion.

"They're only named that because their species

originated in Mexico," she explained. "None of the bats under the bridge are actually Mexican. They were all born right here in Texas."

"Yeah, so was I," Elena replied. "And so was my mama. Do you think that stops some people from calling us Mexicans? Or beaners? Or other even worse names?" She shook her head. "I assure you, it does not."

"I'm sorry," Opal replied. "People who say stuff like that are idiots. Does that happen a lot?"

"It used to," she said. "But it happens a lot less now that we live in Austin. Most folks around here are pretty open-minded. Or they're just plumb crazy, which amounts to the same thing." She smiled over at Opal. "So maybe you'll be able to convince them to let the bats stay after all. It wouldn't be the weirdest thing ever to happen in this city. Not by a long shot."

The four of them talked and talked until the sun went down. When it was finally time for everyone to head home, Elena gave Opal a hug goodbye, and the two of them made plans to hang out together again at Les Amis the following day.

When Uncle Roscoe said goodbye to Maria, she surprised him by giving him a kiss on the cheek and then handing him a piece of paper with her full name and phone number written on it. That was when he found out her last name—*Music*.

"Your last name is Music?" he said. "You're Maria Music?"

She nodded and smiled at him.

"Yes," she said. "Is that okay?"

"Of course!" he replied, laughing nervously. "It's just a weird coincidence, you know. Because I love music." He nudged Opal, who was already turning red with embarrassment. "We both do! Right, Opal?"

Opal grabbed him by the arm and began pulling him toward the exit.

"Come on, Uncle Roscoe," she said. "Time to go home. Say good night."

They said good night to Maria and Elena and started walking home. Halfway there, Opal realized that Uncle Roscoe was still holding the piece of paper Maria had given him with her phone number. He never put it in his pocket. He just continued to clutch it tightly in his hand the entire walk home, as if it were a winning lottery ticket that he was terrified of losing.

Opal and Uncle Roscoe both became regulars at Les Amis. Sometimes they stopped by there several times a day, to eat or to see Maria and Elena. The

food was good, and the company and the people watching were even better. It quickly became their favorite place to hang out, and so Lavaca and Brazos and the rest of the Clothesline Crew started to hang out there a lot, too. And before long, they were also considered regulars.

Maria and the rest of the staff at Les Amis loved having the bats around because they kept all the mosquitoes away from the outside dining area. After the Clothesline Crew filled up on bugs and flew off into the sky, Maria would always wave goodbye to them and shout, "Please come back soon, little bat friends!"

And they did. The bats began to patrol the area around Les Amis whenever it was open, to eat up all the bugs and make things nicer for all the folks who were sitting outside under that awning, eating and laughing and grooving the hours away. And every day, the bats made a few more friends.

17

MAKING AUSTIN WEIRDER

Uncle Roscoe started his part-time job at the newspaper, and then later that week, he also started working part-time at two different RadioShacks on opposites sides of town. From then on, Opal was on her own for several hours each day while her uncle rambled off to work at one of his three jobs.

Opal offered to get a summer job somewhere, too, to help pay their rent, but Uncle Roscoe wouldn't have it.

"You've already got a job," he told her. "It's your job to help the bats fit in here as quickly as possible, so they don't end up facing eviction or destruction. We have to figure out how to get your message out to as many people as possible. *The bats belong beneath the bridge!"*

He gave Opal her own key to the house and told her she was free to go anywhere within a five-mile radius, as long as she left him a note or called to tell him where she was going, and she was always home before it got dark. This wasn't all that unusual for kids her age back then. Her mama had given her a similar amount of freedom to roam her old neighborhood up in Lubbock. But being allowed to wander around the streets of Austin on her own was an entirely different experience. Like having a season pass to a three-ring circus that was always happening right outside her door.

She also had her new friend, Elena, to show her around. Elena would walk Mellow over to Opal's house to hang out every morning after Uncle Roscoe left for work. Mellow would dig holes in the backyard while Opal and Elena used Uncle Roscoe's computer to print out a new stack of THE BATS BELONG BENEATH THE BRIDGE! flyers. Each one had a list of important bat facts listed at the bottom, explaining how many tons of mosquitoes the bats ate every night, noting how helpful they were to farmers, and assuring people that the bats didn't spread rabies or other diseases. The dot-matrix printer would print the flyers out really slow, though, so while they were waiting, Opal and Elena would make additional flyers by hand at the kitchen table while they listened to the radio. Opal would draw a little sketch of Lavaca and Brazos at the bottom of each one.

When they had enough flyers, Opal and Elena would walk Mellow down to the Drag, find an empty street corner, and start handing out their homemade bat flyers to anyone walking by who was interested enough to take one.

Each time they gave someone a flyer, Opal and Elena would shout the slogan printed on it while making a fist to show off the row of four capital letter *B*s printed across their knuckles.

"The bats belong beneath the bridge!" they would shout.

And occasionally, someone would raise their fist and shout it back to them. Every time that happened, it made Opal feel like a million bucks.

INTERESTING AUSTINITES WE MET
WHILE HANDING OUT BAT FLYERS

Aralyn Hughes—Austin's Queen of the Weird. She drives around town in a pink Oldsmobile covered in pig figurines called the pigmobile, with her pet pig, Ara, riding shotgun.

Richard Garriott—A local Austin video game designer who sometimes dresses up in medieval garb and goes by the alias Lord British. He lives outside of town in a mansion filled with secret rooms and passages, and every Halloween he turns it into a haunted house and invites the whole town over to explore it!

Robert Rodriguez—A student at UT and superfriendly guy. He's an artist, just like me and Elena! He draws a really funny comic strip for the student newspaper called *Los Hooligans* that's about a brother and sister who are always getting into trouble. He's saving up money to make his first film, which is going to be called *El Mariachi*.

Mark Bloshock—Mark was so excited to read the flyer we gave him! It turns out he was a Travis County bridge and road

engineer who helped rebuild the Congress Avenue Bridge just before the bats moved in. When he discovered they had accidentally turned it into a perfect bat roost, he promised he would petition the state government to make those same modifications whenever possible to all future bridges built in Texas, whenever possible. How cool would that be?

When they finished handing out all their fly-ers, the girls would usually walk Mellow over to Les Amis and sit at a table outside by the sidewalk while they drew in their sketchbooks.

Opal liked to draw little one-panel cartoons about the Clothesline Crew and all the adventures she imagined they were having when they flew out from under the bridge to find a new collection of musical legends performing around the city each and every night, night after night.

MORE AMAZING MUSICIANS WHO HAVE LIVED IN AUSTIN

Name: Janis Joplin

Birthplace: Port Arthur, Texas

Favorite Songs: Summertime, Piece of My Heart, Me and Bobby McGee

Fun Fact: Lived in a house in Austin known as "The Pink Palace"

Name: Lucinda Williams
Birthplace: Lake Charles, Louisiana
Favorite Songs: Sharp Cutting Wings, Big Red Sun Blues, Sweet Old World

Name: Shawn Colvin
Birthplace: Vermillion, South Dakota
Favorite Songs: Steady On, Ricochet in Time, Polaroids

Elena liked to draw comics. She was currently working on a comic strip titled *Charango*, about a talking armadillo named Charango who was always running around Austin, trying to get away from various musicians who wanted to kill him so they could use the shell on his back to make a rare lute-like musical instrument called a charango that would bring them fame and fortune. It was a really weird comic. Opal loved it.

When Elena's mom, Maria, was working, she would bring free lemonade and grilled cheese sandwiches out to the girls and then stop by every few minutes to compliment them on their drawings. But if the restaurant got busy, she would usually ask them to go hang out at home so her customers could use the table.

One afternoon, Elena was looking over some of Opal's sketches of the Clothesline Crew when she had an idea.

"You should collect all your bat drawings into a zine!" she suggested.

"What's a 'zine'?" Opal replied.

"It's a little photocopied magazine that you make yourself," Elena explained. "And it can be about anything you want. Your zine could be about bats. You could hand it out to people on the Drag to educate them about how friendly and beneficial the bats are." She shrugged. "It might work better than the flyers."

Opal loved the idea, and over the next few days Elena helped her lay out the whole zine and put it together, page by page. They both worked on the interior illustrations, and for the cover, Opal drew a pencil sketch of all the bats flying out from under the bridge at sunset. When everything was ready, Elena took Opal to a place called Kinko's that was filled with dozens of photocopiers, and artists and musicians who were using them to print up flyers for their shows.

With Elena's help, Opal made over three hundred copies of her *Batzine!* She paid for them by breaking open the giant piggy bank she'd been saving in for years. She spent every penny. Then they took their giant stack of Opal's *Batzine!* over to Les Amis and began to hand them out to every customer who came in. Opal was excited because she believed her zine might actually be able to change

the public's opinion of her furry little flying friends, if she could get enough people to read it.

Luckily, one of Les Amis customers they gave a copy to was a man named Louis Black, who happened to be the editor and cofounder of the *Austin Chronicle*, the local independent newspaper. He told Opal and Elena that he loved their zine, and then he asked for permission to reprint some of it in the *Chronicle*, to help spread the word. The girls happily agreed, and just a few days later, when the weekly issue of the *Austin Chronicle* came out, a picture of Opal's *Batzine!* was on the cover, along with her slogan as the headline: *The Bats Belong Beneath the Bridge!* And inside, there was a whole article about the bats, with a picture of Opal and Elena sitting outside and drawing at Les Amis. The article also included blown-up photocopies of all their illustrations from their zine. They were both overjoyed, and Maria and Uncle Roscoe were both incredibly proud of them.

The girls thought the *Austin Chronicle* cover story would fix everything, and that the public's opinion of the bats would change overnight. But it didn't, and this was a rude awakening for both of them. In the days that followed, negative stories calling for the bats to be eradicated continued to appear in other papers and on the local TV news.

It wasn't easy for Opal and Elena to get their hopes up like that, only to immediately have them dashed to pieces. But they decided to view it as a learning experience. From here on out, they had to be realistic. Winning over a few hundred or even a few thousand people wouldn't be enough to save the bats from the forces of certain doom slowly closing in around them. They needed to figure out a way to help the bats win over the entire city, before the entire city turned against them.

The people who live in Austin are called Austinites. And in the weeks that followed, the bats tried to do anything and everything they could think of to win over as many Austinites as possible. They did everything Opal and Uncle Roscoe could think of, too.

Lavaca and Brazos and the rest of the Clothesline Crew split up into pairs again and soared out over the city to scour its streets, searching for people who might want to become their friends and allies.

They flew around to all the outdoor music venues and ate up all the mosquitoes, which made it a lot easier for a lot of folks to enjoy a lot of shows.

They flew around Town Lake and ate up all the

bugs that bothered folks while they were swimming or boating or biking or hiking or riding down the river on paddleboats.

The bats flew out over all the houses, and they ate up all the insects that liked to ruin people's gardens and their picnics at the park.

And while they were eating up all those bothersome bugs, they were doing it to the greatest soundtrack imaginable, grooving to all the best music being performed by all the best musicians from all over the world.

And before too long, all their hard work started to pay off, and the bats began to make some friends....

But they also began to have occasional run-ins with the city's new team of bat catchers, who were constantly on the lookout for them. There had been a few close calls, but so far, the bat catchers hadn't managed to catch a single bat in one of their nets.

Unfortunately, that was about to change.

18

POWERFUL FORCES AND FURRY LITTLE FACES

One morning, Opal and Elena decided to ride along with Uncle Roscoe when he rambled down to his job at the newspaper so that they could visit the bats under the bridge next door. Then they planned to walk up to the state capitol building and hand out bat flyers to as many important-looking people walking around there as they could. This was Elena's idea. She told Opal it would help them spread their message to a lot of powerful people involved in politics, at both the state and local level. Opal thought this was a fantastic idea, and she loaded up her backpack with flyers and the last few copies of her *Batzine!* for the occasion.

It was midmorning when they arrived at the bridge, so nearly all the bats were asleep. But Lavaca and Brazos woke up when they sensed Opal was near, and they both flew out to greet her. Then they followed Opal and Elena as they wandered up Congress Avenue to the big sandstone-colored Texas state capitol building standing at the north end of it, just over a mile from the bridge.

When they reached the capitol building, they discovered that there was a big political rally being held that day, on the grounds in front of the capitol. Opal and Elena walked over to join the huge crowd of onlookers while Lavaca and Brazos roosted in a nearby tree.

The crowd was listening intently to a white-haired lady in a sky-blue suit who was standing up at the podium. Opal didn't know who the woman was, but she really liked what she was saying. Because she was saying that women had been excluded from Texas politics for far too long, and that they deserved a chance to help run the government, too.

Whenever the lady finished a sentence, the crowd would erupt in applause, and Opal and Elena would applaud right along with them. Looking

around, they noticed that several people in the crowd were holding up signs that said ANN RICH-ARDS FOR TEXAS GOVERNOR.

The people in the crowd really seemed to be enjoying what Ann Richards was saying, but a lot of them were having a hard time paying attention to her speech because of all the mosquitoes buzzing around. Opal kept hearing loud slapping sounds throughout the crowd as people attempted to swat mosquitoes that had landed on them.

Opal knew a golden opportunity when she saw one. She nodded at Lavaca and Brazos, and they both flew back to the bridge as quickly as they could. A few minutes later, they returned with a few thousand friends they'd just dragged out of bed. At Opal's direction, the bats ate up all the mosquitoes that were bothering the folks in the crowd. When they were done doing that, they all suddenly flew up and began to swarm around the capitol building itself, where they quickly began to eradicate a massive termite infestation that had only recently been discovered inside the building's majestic dome.

Ann Richards was so grateful to the bats that she asked all her supporters to give them a big round of applause. And they did! Then she went on with her speech.

"This is what I was talking about earlier," Ann Richards told the crowd. "'Be bold, and powerful forces will come to your aid!'"

Opal had never heard that saying before, and she really liked it. So she took her scratchbook out of her backpack and wrote it down inside so she wouldn't forget it. Just as she finished doing this, Opal noticed a really tall, cool-looking red-haired lady standing right beside her, at the back of the crowd. She was wearing a yellow T-shirt that said HOT SAUCE QUEEN on it, and she was scribbling down notes in a notebook, too, while she listened to the speech and studied the crowd. She appeared to be some kind of reporter. But she was also laughing and cheering for Ann Richards along with everyone around her. Opal felt drawn to the woman for some reason.

When Ann Richards finished speaking and left the stage, the crowd erupted in thunderous applause. Then a long line of people who wanted to meet her in person began to form. Opal asked Elena to hold a place in the line for her and then went over to introduce herself to the tall red-haired lady. She was trying to follow the advice Ann Richards had just given her by being bold.

"Hello," Opal said as she walked up to the woman and stuck out her hand. "I'm Opal Flats."

The tall red-haired lady smiled and shook her hand, then she hunkered down to make herself the same height as Opal.

"Well, hello there, Opal Flats!" she replied

cheerfully. "I'm Molly Ivins. It's a pleasure to make your acquaintance."

"Likewise, Molly," Opal said. "I know you're probably working right now, so I don't want to bother you. I just wanted to give you one of these...."

She handed Molly a bat flyer, then showed her the four *B*s she'd drawn across her knuckles with a blue marker earlier that morning.

"*The bats belong beneath the bridge!*" Opal recited.

"They do?" Molly replied, scanning the list of facts at the bottom of the flyer. "I heard that blowhard Muckerno on the city council is angling to get rid of them."

"I know," Opal said. "I'm doing everything I can to stop him. Those bats are my friends. They used to live in a cave nearby my family's farm outside of Comfort, but then Muckerno Limestone destroyed it with dynamite to dig a quarry. Now they've found a new home under the bridge, and Councilman Muckerno is trying to drive them out again, just like his family's company did before. I can't understand why he hates the bats so much."

Molly nodded, listening to all this with increasing interest. Then she raised her notebook and began to write down everything Opal had just said.

"That whole Muckerno clan is about as crooked as a dog's hind leg," Molly said, narrowing her eyes. "You know, they also own a company called Muckerno Chemical that manufactures agricultural pesticides for killing the different bugs that eat up farmers' crops. And your flyer here says that when there's a bat colony nearby, farmers don't need to use any pesticides to kill the bugs, because the bats eat them all up. That could be one reason why Muckerno wants to get rid of the bats and make sure people are afraid of them. It's bad for his business...."

Opal reached into her backpack and took out a copy of her *Batzine!* and handed it to Molly.

"The whole story is in this zine my friend helped me make," Opal said.

"Why, thank you, dear!" she said, flipping through its pages. "I'm going to read this as soon as I get home."

"I hope you dig it," Opal said. "Please help us spread the word if you can."

Molly grinned and nodded.

"I'll see what I can do," she replied as she stood and rose back up to her full height, towering over Opal once again.

"Thanks, Molly!" Opal said as she waved good-bye and ran back over to join Elena in the long line to meet Ms. Richards and shake her hand. By the time they reached the front of it, Opal was really nervous about meeting her, so she let Elena go first. When it was her turn, she summoned her courage and stepped up to the future governor of Texas and put out her hand. Ann Richards smiled wide and shook it.

"Hello, young lady!" she said. "It's so good to see you here. I'm Ann. What's your name?"

"I'm Opal," she said. "It's an honor to meet you! Your speech was really inspiring!"

"Why, thank you, Opal!" she replied. "It's an honor to meet you, too. Thank you for coming out here to support me today."

"You're welcome, Ann," Opal replied. Then she blurted out, "I asked all my bat friends under the bridge to fly over here, too, to eat up all those mosquitoes so everyone could focus on your speech."

Opal was worried Ann might laugh at what she'd just said. But instead, she reached out and gave Opal a big hug.

"I appreciate your help, Opal," she said. "And I appreciate the bats' help, too. Please invite them to come to all my future rallies. I could use the extra mojo!"

Opal's eyes widened in surprise.

"You can count on it, Ann!" she replied. "We've got mojo to spare!"

Ann Richards (politician)

Molly Ivins (newspaper columnist, political commentator, and humorist)

That evening, when Uncle Roscoe got off work, Opal couldn't wait to tell him what had happened at Ann Richards's rally on the capitol lawn earlier that day. But when she did, Uncle Roscoe told her he'd already heard about it from Wiley Woodbern at the paper. The two of them had become friends after Uncle Roscoe trained him on how to use the new word-processing software he'd installed on their office computer systems.

"Wiley is actually an okay guy," Uncle Roscoe said. "He was just misinformed. And he also has a serious phobia of bats. He told me a bat flew into his bedroom once when he was little that scared the living daylights out of him, and he's been terrified of bats ever since. I think that's why he wrote that nasty article about the bats. He was afraid of them."

"*Was* afraid?" she repeated. "But he's not afraid of them anymore?"

Uncle Roscoe smiled wide and nodded.

"Wiley was at that Ann Richards rally today, too," he told her. "He was there covering it for the paper. He told me he froze in terror when all those bats suddenly showed up at the capitol. He couldn't move. Then he watched along with everyone else as they gobbled up all those mosquitoes and termites in a matter of minutes, before disappearing again in a blink. Without harming anyone or infecting anyone with rabies."

"Well, how about that?" Opal replied, a grin spreading across her face.

"Wiley told me he and the other reporters at the paper have been hearing all sorts of positive things about the bats from all sorts of people all over town," Uncle Roscoe said. "He also told me he finally read the copy of your *Batzine!* I gave him, and he loved it! He said it completely changed his opinion of the bats, and that he's already working on a new article about them for the paper to set the record straight. And get this, Opal. He wants to interview you for it! And he'd like to get your permission to use some excerpts from your zine in his article, including a few of your drawings of the Clothesline Crew."

Opal gasped.

"Seriously, dude? My drawings? In the newspaper?"

"Seriously, dude. Your drawings. In the newspaper."

Uncle Roscoe could see what was coming and immediately plugged his ears with his index fingers, just in time to save his eardrums from the assault of Opal's high-pitched squeal of joy, and all the hooting and hollering that followed it.

That was how, with Opal and Uncle Roscoe's help, the bats began to win over the local media. And it was also how Opal and the bats became friends and trusted allies with Ann Richards, one of Austin's most powerful and influential politicians....

After that, the bats started showing up every time Ann Richards held an outdoor campaign event, to clear the area of mosquitoes, red wasps, and blackflies. They made sure no one ever got bothered, bitten, or stung at one of Ann's rallies again. This made them better attended and helped Ann get her message out to more voters.

To show her appreciation, Ann would always mention the bats during her speeches and talk about their benefits to the environment and the community. Then she would recite Opal's slogan and ask her audience to repeat it.

"The bats belong beneath the bridge!" Ann would shout, and then the people would echo it right back to her.

And that was how the word continued to spread, and the tide began to turn.

A few days later, Opal saw a commercial on TV for something called Willie Nelson's Fourth of July Picnic. Uncle Roscoe told her it was a free concert that Willie held for his fans every year, on a big old ranch right outside of town. People came from all over creation to attend, and the turnout got bigger each year.

"Why didn't you tell me about this before, Uncle Roscoe?" Opal said, punching him hard in the shoulder.

"Ow!" he said, laughing. "I don't know. It didn't occur to me."

"I can't believe our luck!" Opal said. "This is the golden opportunity we've been waiting for! Don't you see that? If we win over Willie and all his fans, winning over the rest of the city will be a cinch! And on top of that, Johnny Cash is playing there! We can't miss that!"

She dropped to her knees and clasped her hands together.

"Can we go, Uncle Roscoe?" she pleaded. "Pretty please?"

"Of course we can," he replied, pulling her to her feet. Then he pointed a finger at her and made a serious face. "But don't beg. A Flats never begs. It isn't dignified. Don't ever let me catch you begging again, now, you hear me, girl?"

He tried to tickle her under the ribs, but she squirmed out of his reach. Then she jumped onto his back and wrapped both of her arms around his neck, pretending to put him in a choke hold.

"I beg to differ!" she shouted, tightening her grip. "Now beg me to stop! Beg, old man!"

He began to turn around in circles, feigning confusion.

"Opal?" he said. "Where did she go? Hmm. Well, she appears to have vanished. I sure hope she turns up by the Fourth of July, or I'll just have to go to Willie's picnic without her. Wearing my fancy new necktie."

He walked over to the mirror and pretended to admire the giggling Opal-shaped necktie wrapped around his neck. Then he pretended to find a spot on it.

"Oh no, a stain!" he cried. "I better wash this necktie in the sink!"

When the Fourth of July rolled around, Uncle Roscoe and Opal rambled out to Willie's picnic with Maria and Elena. They got there a little early, to make sure they were among the first people to arrive. And they brought about a million furry little flying friends along with them. (Mellow stayed home. He didn't like crowds.)

Before the show started, Opal asked the bats to fly all around the place, eating up all the flies and mosquitoes that would've done their best to ruin the picnic for everyone, just like they had every previous year it had been held.

Thanks to Opal and the bats, this year's Fourth

of July picnic was different. Not a single person in attendance that day got stung or bit, including all the amazing musicians who appeared onstage with Willie. Including his old friend, the legendary Johnny Cash!

Trinity and Colorado nearly fell out of the sky when they saw him take the stage. They both forgot all about the bugs they were supposed to be eating and flew down to hang from the lighting rig erected above the stage. The two of them stayed there for the rest of the show, both in bat heaven watching Johnny Cash play several of their favorite songs, including "I've Been Everywhere" and "A Boy Named Sue."

Hearing those songs performed live filled Trinity and Colorado up with all kinds of musical mojo, and they beamed all of it right back at the stage, which made Johnny and Willie and everyone else up there play and sing even better, and that made the huge crowd enjoy the music even more.

At the end of the show, Willie Nelson went up to the microphone and declared it to be the best Fourth of July picnic he'd ever had, and he told the

audience that he sure hoped those bug-eating bats would come back again the following Fourth of July, and on every Fourth of July after that.

And that was how the bats became friends with Willie Nelson, one of Austin's most famous and beloved musicians.

(And with Johnny Cash, too!)

After that, things began to get even weirder. It was almost as if Willie had cast some sort of magic spell on Opal and the bats by giving them his blessing on the Fourth of July. Or maybe the extra dose of mojo he gave them that day finally helped them reach a kind of critical mass and permeate the entire city with it. Either way, in the days and weeks that followed, fate continued to weave its own mysterious mojo, by bringing Opal and the bats into contact with all the right Austinites, at just the right time.

For example, one afternoon, Opal was walking along the Drag, taking in all the sights and sounds and passing out flyers, when she spotted a small group of people gathered on the sidewalk out in front of Quackenbush's coffeehouse. (Its full name was Captain Quackenbush's Intergalactic Dessert Company and Espresso Café.) They had just finished laying down what appeared to be a miniature set of train tracks along a section of the sidewalk, and now they were rolling some sort of large contraption up and down them.

When Opal got a little closer, she realized that the machine on the track was a movie camera, and that the people gathered around it were a film crew. Opal recognized them because several of them were regular customers at Les Amis. And two of them were also her neighbors. The guys standing behind the camera, Rick and Lee, lived a few doors down from Opal and Uncle Roscoe, in a house nicknamed "the Fingerhut" because it had a big pointing finger painted on the side of it.

Opal knew that Rick and Lee and their friends were making an independent movie called *Slacker*, because Maria had told her all about it, and Opal had seen the flyers they'd put up along the Drag, inviting people to audition for a role in their film.

Opal watched them make their movie for a little while, until she noticed that a bunch of flies kept flying around in front of their camera lens and buzzing around the actors. This kept screwing up the scene they were filming, which really seemed to upset Rick and Lee, because then they would have to start over and shoot the same thing again. They were wasting a lot of film, which was bad, because film was expensive, and they were on a very low budget.

By now, Opal knew exactly what to do. She summoned Lavaca and Brazos and the rest of the Clothesline Crew and instructed them to follow Rick and Lee around and eat up any bugs that interfered with their film production. This made things a lot easier for the actors who appeared in the movie, and for Lee, who was the cinematographer, and Rick, who was the director.

Opal introduced herself to Rick and explained what she'd done. He was so grateful to Opal for her

help that he gave her a small role in the movie, as a girl selling cans of soda to people on the Drag. He also offered to give her credit on the movie as the official bat wrangler. Opal agreed, but only on the condition that he list the Clothesline Crew in the credits, too, as the movie's official bug wranglers.

And that's how Opal and the bats made friends with Richard Linklater and Lee Daniel and helped out the crew of *Slacker*, one of the best films ever made about Austin and the people who live there.

On another afternoon, Opal was walking along the Drag when she passed by a storefront that had previously been all boarded up. But now all the boards had been taken down, and the place looked all cleaned up. There was also a sign taped to the front window that said COMING SOON: AMY'S ICE CREAMS!

The front door was propped open, and inside the shop Opal saw a woman dancing and sweeping the floor. Opal decided to ask her if she could put a flyer up in her window, but when she stepped inside the store, the woman didn't spot her right away and kept on dancing to the radio. A few seconds later, when she finally *did* spot Opal, she yelped in surprise and jumped about a foot in the air.

"Sorry," she said, once she'd recovered. "I didn't see you there!" She stuck out her hand. "I'm Amy."

"Hi, Amy!" she replied. "I'm Opal."

"It's nice to meet you," Amy said. "But I'm afraid we don't open until sometime next week."

"Oh, that's okay," Opal said. "I was just wondering if it would be okay if I put one of my bat flyers up in your storefront window, so people passing by will see it?"

She handed Amy one of her flyers. Amy scanned it and smiled.

"Of course!" she replied. "I just went down to see the bats for the first time a few nights ago, and watching them fly out at sunset was so beautiful." Her smile suddenly transformed into a scowl as she studied the flyer. "What? I didn't know anyone was trying to get rid of them." She glanced up. "We can't let them do that, Opal! Your flyer is right. *The bats belong beneath the bridge!*"

"I know!" Opal replied, grinning. "Thanks for helping me spread the word."

"My pleasure, Opal," she replied as she took Opal's flyer and taped it to her storefront window. "Let me know if there's anything else I can do to help. And stop by next week after I open, and I'll hook you up with a free double-scoop cone. Deal?"

"Deal!"

And that was how Opal became allies with Amy of Amy's Ice Creams. And when Opal came back the following week, she discovered that Amy had had her slogan printed on all the paper cups and cone sleeves she was selling her ice cream in, right underneath the Amy's Ice Creams logo: *The bats belong beneath the bridge!*

Opal saw it everywhere she looked. There was a huge crowd of people standing around out front, happily devouring their ice cream, and Amy had turned every last one of them into a pro-bat billboard.

Opal could hear Ann Richards's advice echoing in her head. *Be bold, and powerful forces will come to your aid.*

A few days later, Opal and Elena were taking Mellow for a stroll down the Drag when they spotted a man standing on a street corner up ahead who was singing and playing his guitar. When they reached him, they stopped to listen. He was performing a song called "I Live My Broken Dreams," and when he finished singing it, Opal and Elena took all the change in their pockets and dropped it into his open guitar case. He bowed his head in thanks, then knelt down to pet Mellow.

"Hi!" he said, smiling cheerfully. "How are you?"

"We're good," Elena replied. "Thank you for asking."

"My name is Daniel Johnston," he said. "I'm a songwriter. I also work as a janitor at McDonald's."

"Pleased to meet you," Opal replied. "My name is Opal, and this is my friend Elena. And that's Mellow the armadillo." She handed him a flyer. "We're trying to help the bats fit in here."

"Wow! Really?" He studied the flyer for a few seconds, then squinted up at the bright blue sky. "I don't see any bats around."

"Most of them are sleeping right now," Opal told him. "Under the Congress Avenue Bridge downtown."

"That's a good spot," Daniel replied, nodding. "I

slept under that bridge once or twice myself when I first got here. I came to town with the circus and never left."

Daniel took two cassette tapes out of his backpack and handed one to each of them. The label had a drawing of a weird-looking frog on it, along with the words *HI, HOW ARE YOU.*

"That has a bunch of my songs on it," he told them. "It's free."

"Thank you!" Opal replied. She put the tape in her pocket, then handed him a copy of her *Batzine!* "This is our zine about the bats. It's free, too."

Daniel took it, bowing in thanks. Then he stood there and thumbed through it for a few seconds while Opal watched.

"This is so cool!" he said, kneeling down to put the zine in his backpack. "I can't wait to read the whole thing later." Then he stood back up and gave them both a big smile. "Don't worry. Austin isn't like most other places. It's pretty special. If I can fit in here, I bet your bats can, too."

"Thanks, Daniel," Opal replied, returning his smile. "I hope you're right."

When Opal got home, she listened to Daniel's tape and fell in love with his music. But his songs gave her the impression that he might be a little lonely, so she asked the Clothesline Crew to start looking out for him.

From then on, whenever the bats spotted Daniel wandering around the Drag by himself, they would fly down and circle him from above to keep him company. Daniel was always happy to see them, even when he was busy or not in a good mood. And the next time he saw Opal, he told her that he loved having the bats around because he found their presence so relaxing.

* NAME: Daniel Johnston (Born: 1961)

* BEST SONGS: "Walking the Cow," "I Live My Broken Dreams," "Rocket Ship"

* FUN FACT: Daniel called the character in his famous mural "Jeremiah the Frog of Innocence." He took the name from the lyrics of the song "Joy to the World" by Three Dog Night. "Jeremiah was a bullfrog!"

And that was how Opal and the bats became friends with Daniel Johnston.

Later that same week, she and Elena had a similar encounter with a legendary local songwriter named Blaze Foley. They were walking Mellow the armadillo along the Drag when a car backfired, scaring him badly. He lunged in the opposite direction with such force that his homemade collar broke, and he took off running down the street. Most of the people in his way jumped aside, recoiling in terror. But

* **NAME:** Blaze Foley (Born: 1949)

* **BEST SONGS:** "Oval Room," "Wouldn't That Be Nice?" "Clay Pigeons," "Cold, Cold World"

* **FAVORITE THING:** Duct tape. Wears it on his clothes. Uses it to fix stuff.

one tall bearded man stood his ground and stared Mellow down. The sleeves of the jacket he was wearing were wrapped with silver duct tape, and he was using an elastic belt with E.T. printed on it for a hatband.

He grabbed Mellow by the tail and then held him down until Opal and Elena got there. He smiled when they ran up and handed Mellow off to Elena. Then he examined the broken collar hanging at the end of the leash she was holding. He scratched his beard for a moment, then he peeled a long strip of duct tape off his jacket sleeve and wrapped it around Mellow's busted collar a bunch of times, temporarily repairing it. Then he helped Opal and Elena put it back on their armadillo. They both thanked him profusely, but he just nodded and tipped his hat. Then he walked on down the Drag, without ever saying a word.

Opal and Elena didn't even find out who he was until several weeks later, when they saw an article about him in the *Austin Chronicle*. Opal bought a tape of his songs at Waterloo Records and loved all of them, especially one he wrote about the president called "Oval Room" and another one called "Wouldn't That Be Nice?"

. And that was how Opal and Elena and Mellow met Blaze Foley, without even realizing it.

One Saturday night, Uncle Roscoe told Opal he had a special surprise for her. He led her across the Drag, onto the University of Texas campus. They arrived at a tall, brown, windowless building with long ridges all around its exterior. They went inside, and Uncle Roscoe led her through a door labeled STUDIO 6A.

Opal found herself in a big windowless auditorium filled with empty seats and a stage. Behind the stage was a cardboard cutout of the Austin skyline. As soon as Opal saw that, she immediately recognized where they were. The set of *Austin City Limits*! This was the place where they'd recorded all those shows she'd watched on television with her mama, and with Uncle Roscoe and the Clothesline Crew. Now she was going to get to see one of those episodes recorded live! Not only that, but she also realized she was probably going to be *in the episode*, because Uncle Roscoe had called in a favor and gotten them two seats in the center of the front row!

They took their seats in front of the stage just as the rest of the audience began to file in. Opal asked her uncle who was performing that night, but he didn't know. And neither did anyone else in the audience.

"When you buy a ticket to a taping of *Austin City Limits*, you never know who will be playing that night," Uncle Roscoe told her. "You just have to cross your fingers and hope it's someone really good. And it always is."

He smiled and crossed his fingers. Opal smiled back and crossed hers, too. The people sitting around them overheard their conversation, and they all smiled and crossed their fingers, too.

All that finger crossing must've conjured up a whole heaping mess of good luck, because the musician who took the stage that night was the legendary guitarist Stevie Ray Vaughan, backed up by his band, Double Trouble.

Opal just sat there watching them in awe. It was

the best show she had ever seen in her life. At least up to that point.

A little over halfway through their performance, Lavaca and Brazos and the rest of the Clothesline Crew happened to fly over the UT campus during their nightly bug hunt, and when they did, they got close enough to Opal for their telepathic link with her to kick in. For a few seconds they were able to

read her mind, and suddenly they knew where she was and who she was listening to. And this knowledge instantly made all of them go a little crazy. Because now that they knew Stevie Ray Vaughan and Double Trouble were performing on *Austin City Limits* in one of the buildings directly below them, there was no way they could resist trying to sneak into the show.

Brazos found a way into the building through an air-conditioning vent on the roof. Lavaca and the rest of the Clothesline Crew followed him inside, and then they all flew down a series of air ducts, following the sound of Stevie's guitar, until they finally reached the studio where he was playing. One by one, the bats squeezed through the vent and then suspended themselves from the lighting rig directly above the stage to watch the rest of the show.

Opal was so focused on the music that she didn't even realize they were up there. At least, not right away.

The bats all knew they shouldn't do anything to draw attention to themselves, but after listening to the music for a few minutes, they just couldn't resist any longer. Stevie Ray's mojo was just too power-ful, and it made them lose control. Pearl and Sabine adored the blues more than anything, so their will-power evaporated first. They both suddenly took flight and began to circle over the stage, dancing to the mean blues riff Stevie was playing and the lyrics he was singing about his "Pride and Joy."

No one in the audience below seemed to notice them, and this emboldened the other bats enough to join them, one by one, until Lavaca and Brazos were the only remaining holdouts. But then they both threw caution to the wind and joined in, too.

For the remainder of the show, the dancing bats' mojo made the audience enjoy the music even more, and Stevie and his band fed off all that energy, and it made them play the best performance of their lives.

But when the band finished its last song and ran off the stage, several people in the audience finally glanced up and noticed the gang of bats circling directly over their heads. Someone screamed and pointed up at them.

"Bats!" they cried out in horror. Then it suddenly seemed like everyone was screaming all at once.

People began to stampede for the nearest exit, and Opal and Uncle Roscoe were forced to follow them to avoid being trampled.

"Everyone relax!" her uncle shouted. "They won't hurt anyone. They're harmless!"

But no one paid any attention to him. They just kept on running. Just before the stampeding crowd pushed Opal and her uncle out the exit, Opal shouted up at the bats, instructing them to escape by fleeing back outside the same way they'd come in. But as the bats tried to squeeze back into the air vent, they realized it was a lot harder for all of them to squeeze in than it had been for them to squeeze out.

They tried to fly out through one of the exit doors the audience members had used, but as soon as everyone made it outside, the stagehands closed and locked all the doors, trapping the bats inside.

Then they called the bat catchers.

19

MERLIN'S MOJO

By the following morning, the news was all over town. They were talking about it on every radio and TV station Opal tuned into, and it was on the front page of the *Austin American-Statesman* and the *Austin Chronicle*, too. The headlines read: DOUBLE THE BAT TROUBLE! FLYING RODENTS TERRORIZE ACL TAPING OF STEVIE RAY VAUGHAN! CITY COUNCIL IN AN UPROAR!

Opal was devastated. She felt like all her hard work had been ruined in one night, dashing all her hopes for the bats and their future. Worst of all, those bat catchers had captured Lavaca and Brazos and the rest of the Clothesline Crew in their nets and carried them off in cages. Now the bats were all being held prisoner at the humane-society building downtown. And the inhumane jerk working the front desk there wouldn't even let Opal or Uncle Roscoe in to see any of them.

But just as they were about to leave, Opal asked her uncle to drive the Rambler around and park it in back of the building where the bats were being held. When he did as she asked, Opal got close enough to communicate telepathically with Lavaca, and she asked her to tell Brazos and all the other bats being held inside not to worry, because she and her uncle were going to figure out a way to free them. She promised.

But when they got home and Uncle Roscoe turned on the news, Opal immediately began to wonder if she was going to be able to keep her promise.

Councilman Muckerno was already using all the negative press about the bats to pressure the city government into eradicating them once and for all. He appeared to be telling every newspaper, radio, and TV reporter who would listen that the city of

Austin wouldn't be safe again until every last bat was banished from the bridge and from the city as a whole. He claimed he'd already spoken with the public works department about securing enough blowtorches and flamethrowers to force all those "flying rodents" out of the narrow cracks on the underside of the bridge they were hiding in. Once the bats were gone, Muckerno said they would cover all the cracks with wire screens to prevent them from ever getting back in again.

Muckerno said he would move forward with his plan as soon as the city council voted to approve it, which he hoped would happen at their next weekly meeting.

Opal and Uncle Roscoe spent the rest of the day pacing back and forth in their living room, trying to come up with a new plan. But they'd already tried everything they could think of to help the bats win over the people of Austin, and it just hadn't been enough. They both felt like giving up, but neither one of them was willing to admit it to the other.

That night, when bedtime rolled around, Opal and Uncle Roscoe were both still too worried about the bats to fall asleep, so they stayed up way past midnight watching TV on the couch in their tiny living room.

Late Night with David Letterman happened to be on, and that was when they finally had a stroke of good luck. Because one of the guests on the show that evening was a fellow by the name of Merlin Tuttle. He was a bat conservationist who lived up in Wisconsin.

He told Dave he'd been fascinated by bats ever since he was a little boy. That was why he'd devoted his life and career to protecting them, by educating people about how beneficial they were to the environment.

He even brought a little bat on the show with him, so he could show the audience and the TV cameras how friendly and cute it was up close.

When Merlin's interview ended and they cut to a commercial, Opal and Uncle Roscoe stared at each other for a moment in disbelief. Then, without saying a word, they both jumped up and ran to the phone.

It took some time, but eventually they were able to get Merlin's home number from the operator. Then they called him up. And to their surprise, he answered the phone, even though it was the middle of the night.

Uncle Roscoe handed the phone to Opal, who told Merlin an abbreviated version of her story— the same story I've been telling you.

As soon as Merlin heard that an entire colony of Mexican free-tailed bats had taken up residence in downtown Austin, less than a mile from the Texas state capitol, he knew this was the golden opportunity he'd been waiting for his entire life. This was his chance to prove that bats could live alongside humans in perfect harmony—and he wasn't going to miss out on it.

After Merlin got off the phone with Opal, he didn't even wait until morning to leave. He packed everything he owned into his car that very night and hit the road for Austin. There wasn't a moment to spare.

It took Merlin a whole day of driving before he reached Austin. As soon as he arrived, he called up Opal and Uncle Roscoe, and they rambled down to meet him. Then Opal introduced Merlin to the bats who were still free and told them they could trust him. Then Opal and her uncle took Merlin out for barbecue and they formulated a plan to free the Clothesline Crew.

The very next morning, Merlin sprang into action. First, he went to the humane society, and because he was a famous environmentalist who had just appeared on *Letterman* earlier that week, he was able to persuade the mean old bat catchers to release the Clothesline Crew into his custody.

Then he brought all twelve of the bats to the Austin City Council meeting being held that night. Opal and Uncle Roscoe helped him carry their cages in. Merlin opened them up one at a time, and then he let the people on the council pet each of the bats and see how cute they were up close. Once the people on the council realized that the furry little critters under the bridge weren't anything like the rabid vampire bats depicted in horror movies, their opinion of the bats slowly began to change.

"The bats under the bridge are making this city a better place to live," Merlin explained. "By eating tens of thousands of insects every night, including mosquitoes that spread disease." He also explained how the bats were saving local farmers millions of dollars a year by protecting their crops, while also preventing the need for them to use harmful chemical pesticides.

But it didn't matter what Merlin said. Councilman Muckerno wouldn't budge.

"I don't care how friendly or beneficial or cute

those bats are!" he told Merlin. "They're a serious health concern and a public nuisance! If we let them stay where they are, they'll scare away visitors and ruin the local tourist industry. I want them gone, and a lot of other people in town feel the same way."

He ended his tirade by pointing out that, according to a poll conducted by the *Austin American-Statesman* newspaper, there were almost as many people who hated the bats and wanted them to leave as there were people who loved them and wanted them to stay.

The city council finally decided to hold a special citywide vote called a referendum to let the citizens of Austin choose whether the bats should stay or go. And the evening before the voting was set to take place, they held a big public debate at the state capitol building downtown to decide their fate....

Opal and Uncle Roscoe and Maria and Elena told everyone they knew about it, and they handed out flyers to people up and down the Drag, asking everyone to attend the debate and speak in defense of the bats.

But when the time came, Opal wasn't sure if anyone would actually show up.

20

THE SHOWDOWN DOWNTOWN

Opal didn't have anything to worry about. When the evening of the big debate arrived, hundreds of people from all over Austin crowded into the state capitol building to watch it. And thousands of other people were watching at home because the event was also being broadcast live on ACTV, the local public access television station.

Merlin, Opal, Uncle Roscoe, Maria, and Elena were all seated in the front row. Opal wore her turquoise tuxedo, because she figured wearing something her mama had made for her might give her some extra mojo. Uncle Roscoe wore his gemstone jean jacket for the same reason.

Lavaca and Brazos and the rest of the Clothes-line Crew were there to watch the big debate, too, though no one, including Opal, knew it. In fact, she'd expressly forbidden the bats to attend. That was why they were hanging high up in the rafters way at the back of the room. They hated defying Opal, but they couldn't help themselves. They didn't want to miss anything! And because they assumed there wouldn't be any live music being performed during the debate, the Clothesline Crew figured it would be easy for them to keep quiet and stay out of sight during the proceedings.

As soon as the moderator opened the floor for debate, Councilman Muckerno was the first one up to the podium. He scowled down at Opal and Merlin and all the bat lovers in the crowd. Then he delivered a long, loud, angry speech about how the bats were "flying rodents" who "spread rabies everywhere" and "attacked innocent citizens in the street." He told the people of Austin that they had to get rid of the "Congress Avenue Cauldron" to ensure the public health and safety of their children.

"If the bats are allowed to stay," he proclaimed,

"we might as well change the name of this city to Transylvania, Texas!"

By the time Councilman Muckerno had finished spewing all that misinformation, the people in the audience who had already been afraid of bats were now absolutely terrified of them.

The moderator called for a rebuttal.

Opal glanced down at the crumpled piece of paper in her hands. She'd spent hours writing out her own speech in defense of the bats. But now that the time had come to get up and deliver it, she suddenly had a serious case of stage fright. If she went up there in front of all these people right now, she would be too petrified to speak. But no one else was walking up to the podium, and for a few terrible seconds it seemed like no one was going to come to the bats' defense.

She turned to find Merlin, because he'd promised to get up and speak. But his seat was empty. He seemed to have disappeared. For a moment she wondered if he might be suffering from stage fright, too. Then she spotted him up on the stage, already making his way to the podium!

Opal was a little worried because he didn't appear to have anything written down. When he reached the podium, he pushed a few buttons on it, and a fancy projector screen lowered from the ceiling behind him. Then all the lights dimmed, and a picture of a big old beautiful mess of bats appeared on the screen. They were all hanging upside down from the roof of a big old beautiful cave. It looked a lot like the one Opal's bats used to live in, but it wasn't the same one.

In a calm and friendly voice, Merlin began to explain how the bats lived and what their families were like, and the role they played in maintaining

the balance of nature. It turned out Opal needn't have worried, because Merlin had been memorizing bat facts his entire life, and he'd come to this debate prepared with a whole slideshow.

He showed a lot of other cute close-up photos of bats going about their business, while he laid out all the reasons why the people of Austin should welcome the bats roosting under the bridge instead of forcing them to leave. He explained how they improved the local ecosystem and how much they helped all the local gardeners and farmers and business owners and outdoor music venues. Then he showed some pictures Opal had given him of the dozens of folks who had started to gather on the Congress Avenue Bridge every night at sunset to lean over the railing and watch the bats emerge for the evening.

When the lights came back up, everyone gave Merlin a huge round of applause. Opal and Uncle Roscoe and Maria and Elena applauded harder than anyone else. Then, to Opal and her uncle's surprise, Maria and Elena both jumped to their feet and ran up to the podium together! Maria told everyone about all the help the bats had given her restaurant by getting rid of all the mosquitoes and flies that used to harass the customers who sat outdoors. Then Elena reached into her satchel and pulled out a whole bunch of new copies of the *Batzine!* she'd made the day before at Kinko's, without Opal even knowing about it. She handed a zine to the debate moderator, and to every member of the city council, including Councilman Muckerno. He threw his copy on the floor.

Opal heard everyone on the city council gasp—not because of what Muckerno had done, but because now Ann Richards was walking up to the podium! She still hadn't been elected governor quite yet, but she was already the state treasurer, so everyone knew who she was. Still, she introduced herself anyway. Then she walked over and picked up the copy of Opal's zine Muckerno had thrown on the floor and put it into her pocket.

"You know why I think Councilman Muckerno hates those bats so much?" she asked the crowd. "Because they're so much better at making friends than he is! And I think they might have a better barber to boot."

That made everyone within earshot bust out laughing. Everyone but Councilman Muckerno, who turned as red as a beet and reached up to self-consciously check his hair. He had both a comb-over and a cowlick, and it wasn't a flattering combination.

Ann Richards told everyone how the bats had improved attendance at all her political rallies by eating up all the mosquitoes that had kept folks away. She also told them how the bats had already saved the state government by gobbling up the termite infestation that could've seriously damaged the capitol building. Finally, she said that when she became governor, she would do everything in her power to protect the bats beneath the bridge.

"Now I want to bring up a very old friend of mine," Ann Richards told the crowd. "Her name is Molly Ivins, and she's learned something you should all know."

Molly Ivins walked up to the podium, high-fiving Ann Richards as she stepped away from it.

"I just thought everyone here would like to know that the reason these bats showed up here in Austin in the first place is because their natural habitat was destroyed when Muckerno Limestone dynamited their cave to build a new quarry. And yes, that company is owned by Councilman Muckerno's family. He and all his siblings and cousins sit on the board of directors!"

There were gasps throughout the crowd. Then people began to boo and hiss at the councilman, who was beginning to squirm in his seat.

"They also own a company called Muckerno Chemical that manufactures chemical pesticides, which farmers don't need if there are bats around," Molly added, pointing a finger at Councilman Muckerno. "That's why he doesn't want any bats around! And he's willing to lie to the entire city to get rid of them!"

Now the entire audience was booing at Muckerno, but he refused to leave.

As Molly and Ann left the stage to thunderous applause, a broad-shouldered man that Opal didn't recognize made his way to the podium. He was wearing a burnt-orange Longhorns windbreaker. Her uncle whispered that he was the coach of the UT football team. He didn't really give a speech. It was more like he just started chewing everyone in the audience out. The same way he would a locker room full of football players for acting foolish out on the field. He didn't even bother using the microphone. He just yelled at everyone, including the city council members up on stage with him.

"Y'all need to wise up and leave those bats alone!" he shouted. "Didn't anyone think this through? When football season starts in a few weeks, those bats are gonna make all of my team's upcoming practices and games a lot more bearable by eating up the millions of mosquitoes that always show up to plague my players and all of our fans up in the stands! I can't believe I have to come down here and explain this to all of you, like a bunch of third graders." He pointed an angry finger at the crowd, then turned to point it at the members of the city council. "Now get your act together, all of you, and do the right thing. Or you will all incur my wrath. Got it?"

No one said a word. You could've heard a pin drop. When Opal glanced around, everyone appeared to be holding their breath.

As the coach walked off the stage, he suddenly raised his right hand and made a fist, and for a second Opal was worried he might sock someone, but instead he turned it toward the crowd to show everyone the four *B*s written across his knuckles.

"The bats belong beneath the bridge!" he shouted, and the crowd went wild.

Just as the commotion began to die down a little, Rick Linklater emerged from the audience and walked up to the podium. He politely introduced himself as a local independent filmmaker and then told everyone how the bats had helped out the cast and crew of *Slacker* by bug wrangling all the mosquitoes trying to sabotage the making of their movie. Then he pointed out Opal in the front row.

"I'd also like to thank my friend Opal there, for being our bat wrangler," he said, raising a copy of her *Batzine!* high over his head. "And I also want to commend her for having the courage to exercise her First Amendment rights to freedom of speech and freedom of the press to do battle with our local bureaucracy and challenge the lies of their puppets in the media, by delivering the truth directly into the hands of the people. Rock on, little sister! The bats belong beneath the bridge!"

He gave her a thumbs-up as he left the stage, and the entire audience erupted into applause. That gave Opal a big dose of courage, and before she knew what was happening, *she* was walking up to the podium. But when she got up there, she wasn't quite tall enough to see over it. So she took the microphone off its stand and stepped out from behind the podium. Then she raised the mic to her lips and the words suddenly began to pour out of her. She told everyone about how the bats used to be her neighbors and how they protected all of the farmers' crops, by eating up all the bugs intent on ruining their harvests. Then she told everyone how the bats were driven out of their previous home in the big old beautiful cave by humans with bulldozers and dynamite.

"I think it'd be mighty cruel for y'all to force the bats out of their new home under the bridge," Opal said, eyeing Councilman Muckerno out of the corner of her eye. "Seeing as how human greed was what destroyed their original home in the first place."

Then, before she left the stage, she said one last thing.

"Besides, isn't Austin supposed to be the city where weirdos are welcome?" she asked. "Well, what could be weirder than a whole big mess of a million beautiful music-loving bats living under a bridge downtown?"

She raised both her fists, brandishing the four Bs scrawled across the front of each of them, and shouted, "The bats belong beneath the bridge!" as she left the stage.

The audience burst into applause. Opal hurried back to her seat, blushing from all the compliments folks were giving her as she passed them. And when she got there, Uncle Roscoe threw his arms around her and hugged her tight. Then Maria and Elena appeared and hugged both of them.

"We're so proud of you, Opal," Uncle Roscoe said.

Before she could respond, a bunch of the people sitting near the entrance gasped. Then a lot of other people in the crowd began to jump to their feet, clapping and cheering. A few seconds later, Opal was able to see why. It was because Willie Nelson himself was sauntering up to the podium. And he was carrying his battered and beat-up old guitar, Trigger!

Willie spent a few minutes tuning it while he told the crowd how the bats had eaten up all the mosquitoes at his annual Fourth of July picnic and that, as a result, it was easily the best Fourth of July picnic they'd ever had. Then he said he wanted to play a song the bats had inspired him to show up and sing, called "Blue Skies."

As soon as Willie started singing and strumming, everyone heard a commotion coming from somewhere above, high up in the rafters. It was the Clothesline Crew! The sound of Willie singing and strumming on Trigger was too beautiful for them to resist! They all took flight and began to circle above Willie, flapping their little wings in time with the song.

For a few seconds, Opal worried the sight of the bats might cause another stampede. But it didn't! No one screamed or ran. Because no one there was afraid of the bats anymore, thanks to everything they'd just seen and heard, and thanks to what they were seeing and hearing with their own eyes and ears right now—Willie Nelson singing a song to a dozen melomaniac bats who were dancing in the air over his head, filling up the whole place with so much mojo it was coming out all the windows.

Willie's song had most of the audience tearing up by the time he'd finished singing it. Including Maria and Elena and Opal and Uncle Roscoe. And Merlin Tuttle, too.

When Willie finished singing, everyone in the audience began to cheer and applaud. Then Willie leaned into the microphone and started a chant

that quickly spread through the crowd: *"The bats belong beneath the bridge! The bats belong beneath the bridge!"*

Before long, every single person in the place was chanting it. Except, of course, Councilman Muckerno, who simply got up and walked out of the chamber with his head down as the crowd continued to chant around him.

Opal didn't know it yet, but at that moment, Willie's chant was spreading across the entire city. Everyone listening to the debate on the radio or watching on the TV at home or in some coffee shop or record store or dance hall or honky-tonk was also starting to chant, *"The bats belong beneath the bridge! The bats belong beneath the bridge!"*

For a few minutes, you could hear those words being chanted all over town.

And the next day, when the vote was held, the people of Austin decided by an overwhelming majority to let the bats remain in their new home under the Congress Avenue Bridge forever.

That was the moment when Opal decided she wanted to live in Austin forever, too.

21

THE BIG OLD BEAUTIFUL BRIDGE

There. Now y'all have heard the whole wild and weird tale of how a million Mexican free-tailed bats came to live under the Congress Avenue Bridge over Town Lake.

In the months and years that followed, the bats under the bridge became the city's beloved mascots. The mayor eventually decided to declare Austin the Bat Capital of America, in addition to it already being the Texas state capital and the Live Music Capital of the World. That seems like an awful lot of capitals for one town, but anything that makes folks happy is fine with me.

Speaking of making folks happy, the coach of

the UT football team was right. When the bats all started to show up at the stadium for the Longhorns' home games, they would eat up all the moths and mosquitoes that would usually prevent folks from enjoying the Friday night lights. The bats were a literal game-changer, and the extra mojo they gave the team helped the Longhorns kick off a winning streak that lasted all season long. The Clothesline Crew even made friends with Bevo the Eighth, the longhorn bull who served as the team's mascot. During home games, you could always find them hanging out with him.

The bat colony under the bridge became one of Austin's biggest tourist attractions. Nowadays, millions of folks come here every year, just to stand on top of the Congress Avenue Bridge and watch all those bats fly out over Town Lake each night. It's a real sight to see. And now you can even have dinner floating on a boat while you see it, if you have the inclination.

A few years back, the city decided to rename it the Ann W. Richards Congress Avenue Bridge, after our illustrious former governor. They also decided to stop calling it Town Lake and rename it Lady Bird Lake after President Johnson's wife. But the bats didn't seem to mind.

To show their love and appreciation, the people of Austin even erected a statue of a bat downtown, just a few blocks from the statues we built to honor Willie Nelson and Stevie Ray Vaughan.

And get this: Now, once every year, they block

off traffic to the bat bridge to hold the city's annual Bat Fest on top of it, to celebrate how much the people of Austin have grown to adore having the bats as their neighbors.

Can you believe how things turned out? For a while there, people were seriously talking about burning the bats out from under that bridge with blowtorches and flamethrowers. Now they get treated like royalty. Because folks around here know Austin just wouldn't be Austin anymore without all those furry little flying critters living under that big old beautiful bridge downtown.

It has to be the only time in history that a million critters ever relocated to the center of a major American city, unintentionally terrorized its citizens, and were subsequently declared an invasive species and a threat to public health, only to end up as the city's beloved mascots and one of its most popular tourist attractions just a few years later. I mean, where else in the world could something like this have happened?

Only in Austin.

In the end, Pearl and Sabine, Rainey and Red, Koenig and Lamar, Cesar and Jacinto, Trinity and Colorado, and Lavaca and Brazos all found the perfect home for themselves and their entire enormous bat family. And I can personally assure you that each and every one of them lived happily ever after.

Don't worry. Opal lived happily ever after, too. How would I know? Because, dear reader, as you may have guessed by now, I'm her, and she's me. I was just telling y'all this story in the third person to keep you in suspense about how things worked out for that weird little barrel-shaped girl that I used to be. But now I don't mind telling y'all that everything worked out for her just fine.

After the wildest and weirdest summer any girl could ever have, I started attending O. Henry Middle School in the fall, which was the same school Elena went to. That made going there a lot less frightening, since I knew I already had at least one friend. Even so, the Clothesline Crew showed up on my first day, circling over the playground to make sure I didn't feel lonesome during recess. But they didn't need to worry, because I had my pal Elena with me. And once I got to know the other kids in my class a little, I discovered that most of them had a mile-wide weird streak in them, too, just like the two of us. We were all a bunch of weird kids with weird teachers at a weird school in the weirdest town in Texas. Where no one ever ends up being labeled a misfit because everyone is some sort of misfit, so all the misfits fit right in.

Uncle Roscoe went back to school the same week I did, to study computer engineering at UT just like he'd always dreamed. He became really good friends with one of his classmates, a guy named Michael Dell, and helped him start a business building computers in his dorm room. After graduation, Uncle Roscoe went to work for him at his new company, which eventually became Dell Computer Corporation. He also asked Maria to marry him, and that was when she became Aunt Maria, and Elena and I became cousins. And when we all moved into a new house together, Mellow became our armadillo, too. The three of them made our weird little family complete.

Merlin decided to stay in Austin, too. He founded an organization here called Merlin Tuttle's Bat Conservation to research and protect bats all over the world, and to help educate people about them. He inspired me to study bat conservation at UT, and after I graduated, I went to work for the Texas Parks and Wildlife Department. Now I get paid to stand under the bridge every night at sunset and tell folks all sorts of weird and interesting facts about the bats and their unique home. It's the best job in the world. Millions of people come here every year from all over the world to see my furry little friends fly out from under that bridge, and when they finally do, it never fails to put smiles on their faces or the bats in their good graces. It's like some strange kind of magic that just never seems to run out.

Elena and I have both also become minor celebrities, thanks to a popular comic strip we cocreated called *Big City Bats* that appears every week in the *Austin Chronicle*. The main characters are all based on our furry little friends in the Clothesline Crew, so they're all local celebrities now, too.

I've never seen another flying saucer. Not since that night at the farm. Not yet, anyway. I still don't know what it was, where it came from, or why it gave me the ability to communicate with the bats. But that ability has never gone away, thankfully. I can still talk to them whenever I need to, and vice versa. I'm always going to be here for them, and I know they're always going to be here for me. Because we're family. And we stick together, through thick and thin, frown or grin, until we win.

If you want my opinion, I think it was probably my mama up there with the Spirit in the Sky orchestrating everything. I think she led me to the bats, and then she led all of us to Austin. Because somehow she knew we needed one another, and that Austin needed us.

I can't prove it. But that's what I think.

I've changed an awful lot since those days, and so has Austin. A bunch of the people and places I mentioned in my story aren't around anymore. But a few of them still are. The bats are still here. So is Merlin. So are Uncle Roscoe and Aunt Maria and my cousin

Elena. And so am I. And all of us bat-loving meloma-niacs are still living it up down here in the Groover's Paradise. Eating *all* the best tacos and *all* the best barbecue while we listen to *all* the best music being performed by *all* the best musicians from *all* over the world pretty much *all* the time. While all our furry little flying friends under the bridge handle the mosquitoes.

Y'all should come on down here sometime and pay us a visit.

Afterword

After reading this "mostly true tall tale," some of you may be wondering which parts of the story really happened and what inspired me to write it in the first place. If so, then you're in luck, because I know the answers to both of those questions, and I'm fixin' to share them with you right now, here in this afterword.

I moved to Austin from my home state of Ohio in the mid-nineties, drawn by the city's unique personality and warm climate. The small Texas town had somehow become a magnet for musicians, filmmakers, artists, slackers, and all manner of misfits, who were constantly moving there in droves from all over the state and the country. That was one of the many reasons the city's motto was "Keep Austin Weird."

It seemed like the kind of place where I would

fit right in, and I did. Austin quickly became my favorite city. Driving through its streets each evening, my ears were treated to all genres of music being performed by all sorts of amazing musicians from all over the world. To a guy from a small town in Ohio, it felt like I'd wandered onto the set of some kind of international multicultural jukebox musical being staged on the streets all around me— twenty-four hours a day, seven days a week, all year long.

I'd only been living here for a few days when I first heard about the bats beneath the bridge. Whenever a local found out I was new in town, they would often ask if I'd "gone to see the bats yet." When I said no, they would always shake their heads and reply, "Aw, man! You gotta go see the bats!"

To my surprise, I learned that Austin was home to the world's largest urban bat colony. Over a million Mexican free-tailed bats were living under the Congress Avenue Bridge in the heart of downtown, just a few blocks south of the state capitol building. And every evening at dusk, hundreds of people would gather on the bridge to watch the bats stream out from under it and fly up in one long, beautiful, undulating murmuration that filled the sky overhead.

The evening I first witnessed this spectacle proved to be one of the most exhilarating—and inspiring—moments of my life. Ever since then, my imagination has continued to wander back to these captivating creatures. Where did these bats come from? How did they end up in Austin? What led to their fame? What challenges did they face on their journey here? What sort of personalities might they have? Did this giant family of bats have anything in common with mine?

As time went on, I learned more about the fantastic true history of Austin's bridge bats, and it inspired me even more.

Here's what really happened:

Way back in 1982, the Texas Transportation Department finished upgrading the old Congress Avenue Bridge. It was rebuilt with concrete box beams that were each separated by a narrow crevice to allow for heat expansion. These crevices were a foot and a half deep and they unintentionally created an ideal roost for migrating Mexican free-tailed bats, which need dark, warm, narrow habitats where they can sleep during the day and nurse their pups in safety.

Before long, a group of bats took up residence in these crevices under the bridge. This colony grew each year by the hundreds of thousands of bats, and by 1984, its population had grown to nearly a million.

The sudden arrival of the bats caused a panic in the capital city. Local newspapers began to run sensational articles with headlines like *Bats Invade Austin!* and *Bat Colonies Sink Teeth into City!*

A few of the more alarmed Austinites began to petition the city council to eradicate the bats. Several local officials declared them to be a public health hazard. Plans were made to capture the bats with nets and there were discussions about using blowtorches to burn them out of their new home under the bridge. The city also proposed covering those crevices on the underside of the bridge with wire mesh to prevent bats from roosting there again in the future.

Luckily, not everyone agreed that the bat colony under the bridge presented a danger. One of these people was a young bat advocate from Wisconsin named Merlin Tuttle, who had read about the plight of the Austin bats in national news coverage. To Merlin, the Texas state capital's unwelcome bat colony presented a unique opportunity. So he quit his day job as Curator of Mammals at the Milwaukee Public Museum and moved down to Austin to try and help prevent the bats from being driven out of their new home.

And then something magical happened. The bats slowly began to win over the people of Austin. Many Austinites were surprised to learn that the bat colony ate several tons of disease-spreading mosquitoes every night, which everyone appreciated. During the summer, a third or more of the bridge bats' diet came from moths, including North America's number one agricultural pest, the earworm moth, known for decimating corn and tomato crops and devouring a wide variety of fruits and vegetables, which made every Austinite with a garden or farm thankful for the bats.

Thanks to a combination of the bats' positive impact on the local ecosystem and the counterculture sensibility of Austin's unique mix of artists, musicians, and open-minded outlaws, public opinion of the bats gradually began to change. Because—like me and so many other weirdos who moved to Austin—those furry little flying critters fit right in here. In a city that prided itself on being weird, the bats somehow made the perfect addition to the local landscape. Because what could be weirder than a million bats living under an old bridge downtown?

By 1989, the city government had completely reversed its position, and they voted to let the bats stay in their new home under the bridge. Then they began to pass a series of laws designed to protect the bats and their habitat. And on April 20, 1990, a special ceremony was held beneath the bridge to honor the bats. The mayor got up and proudly declared that Austin was now "the Bat Capital of America."

And that's how, in a span of just eight years, the bats went from being branded a public nuisance to being anointed the city's beloved mascots—while also becoming one of its main tourist attractions.

These days, millions of people visit Austin every year just to see our bats, which generates millions of dollars in tourist revenue for local businesses.

I was fascinated by this weird and wild tale, because it organically included important themes about the environment and the benefits of living alongside those very different from ourselves. I also saw how the true elements of the bats' story could serve as the basis for a heartwarming tall tale about a lovable group of misfits who relocate to a new place and try to make a home for themselves among strangers who are predisposed to fear their kind.

After my kids were born, I enjoyed telling them bedtime stories that merged real facts about the bats with a fictional backstory I'd imagined for them. I set this "mostly true tall tale" in the idealized "Old Austin" of the 1980s I always heard people reminiscing about, and to make my tale extra tall, I condensed a decade's worth of history into one "wild and weird summer" that I filled with all sorts of fudged facts and outlandish anachronisms.

Over the years, the story I'd concocted about Opal B Flats and the Austin bridge bats always stayed with me, roosting in the back of my imagination. I knew someday I had to write it all down in a book, so that parents and kids everywhere could enjoy my urban fable about Opal and the bats, too.

Now you hold that book in your hands. And I hope you enjoyed reading it as much as I did writing it.

Sincerely,
Ernest Cline
Austin, Texas
April 26, 2023

Acknowledgments

I never could have written this story without all the love, encouragement, and inspiration provided by my fabulous wife, Cristin O'Keefe Aptowicz, and our two amazing kids, Libby and Maureen.

I'm also extremely grateful to Mishka Westell for her beautiful illustrations, and to Ramona Kaulitzki for her gorgeous cover artwork.

My heartfelt gratitude also goes out to my incredible literary agent, Yfat Reiss Gendell; my tireless manager and producing partner, Dan Farah; my wonderful editor, Alvina Ling; and all the other kind and daring souls at Little, Brown and Company, including Lily Choi, Crystal Castro, Jackie Engel, and Megan Tingley.

I'm also extremely grateful to my incredibly talented friend (and former Austinite) Felicia Day for narrating the audiobook.

I also owe a big thank-you to Merlin Tuttle, for

inspiring me with his words and deeds, and for answering my endless questions about bats. I also want to express my appreciation to all the musicians, filmmakers, writers, orators, and artists whose work I've paid tribute to in this tall tale of mine. They've all entertained and enlightened me over the years, and I hope that this story will inspire others to seek out their creations.

Finally, I want to thank you, dear reader, for coming along on another adventure with me.

BRIDGE TO BAT CITY SOUNDTRACK:

1. Boogie Back to Texas: Asleep at the Wheel
2. Rave On: Buddy Holly
3. Spirit in the Sky: Norman Greenbaum
4. On the Road to Find Out: Yusuf Islam (Cat Stevens)
5. One Time, One Night: Los Lobos
6. Not Fade Away: Buddy Holly
7. Jack Gets Up: Leo Kottke
8. Got My Mojo Working: Muddy Waters

9. You're Gonna Miss Me: 13th Floor Elevators
10. I Believe I'm in Love: The Fabulous Thunderbirds
11. Cliffs of Dover: Eric Johnson
12. Como la Flor: Selena
13. Musta Notta Gotta Lotta: Joe Ely
14. This Must Be the Place (Naive Melody): Talking Heads
15. Mess Around: Ray Charles
16. Big Cheeseburgers and Good French Fries: Blaze Foley
17. Gimme All Your Lovin': ZZ Top
18. Pride and Joy: Stevie Ray Vaughan
19. Piece of My Heart: Janis Joplin
20. Think It Over: Buddy Holly
21. Blue Skies: Willie Nelson

Bonus Track. Feelin' Good Again: Robert Earl Keen

Dan Winters

ERNEST CLINE

is a #1 *New York Times* bestselling novelist, screenwriter, father, and full-time geek. He is the author of the novels *Ready Player One*, *Ready Player Two*, and *Armada*, and co-screenwriter of the film adaptation of *Ready Player One*, directed by Steven Spielberg. His books have been published in over fifty countries and have spent more than one hundred weeks on the *New York Times* bestsellers list. He lives in Austin, Texas, with his family, a time-traveling DeLorean, and a large collection of classic video games. *Bridge to Bat City* is his debut middle-grade novel.